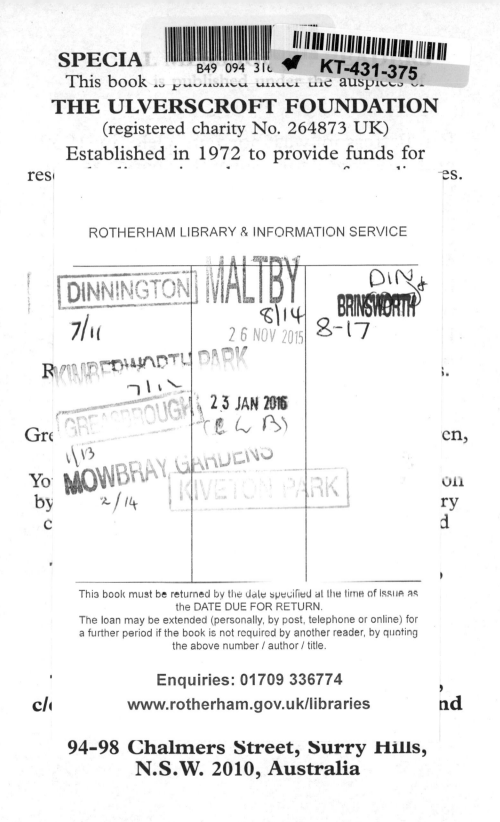

Per Petterson was born in Oslo in 1952 and worked for several years as an unskilled labourer, a bookseller, a writer and a translator. He made his literary breakthrough in 2003 with the novel *Out Stealing Horses*, which has been translated into 40 languages so far and won many prizes, including the International IMPAC Dublin Literary Award and the *Independent* Foreign Fiction Prize.

I CURSE THE RIVER OF TIME

It is 1989 and all over Europe Communism is crumbling. Arvid Jansen, thirty-seven, is in the throes of a divorce. At the same time, his mother is diagnosed with cancer. Over a few intense autumn days, we follow Arvid as he struggles to find a new footing in his life, while all the established patterns around him are changing at staggering speed. As he attempts to negotiate the present, he casts his mind back to holidays on the beach with his brothers, to courtship, and to his early working life, when as a young Communist he abandoned his studies to work on a production line.

Books by Per Petterson
Published by The House of Ulverscroft:

OUT STEALING HORSES

PER PETTERSON

I CURSE THE RIVER OF TIME

Translated from the Norwegian
by

Charlotte Barslund
with Per Petterson

Complete and Unabridged

ULVERSCROFT
Leicester

First published in Great Britain in 2010 by
Harvill Secker, London

First Large Print Edition
published 2011
by arrangement with
Harvell Secker
The Random House Group Limited, London

First published with the title *Jeg forbanner tidens elv*
in 2008 by Forlaget Oktober, Oslo

British Library CIP Data

Petterson, Per, *1952* –
  I curse the river of time.
  1. Communists- -Fiction. 2. Mothers and sons- -
  Fiction. 3. Life change events- -Fiction. 4. Europe- -
  Politics and government- -*1989*- -Fiction.
  5. Large type books.
  I. Title
  839.8'2374–dc22

  ISBN 978–1–4448–0718–9

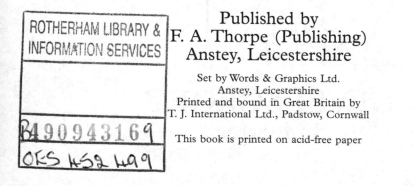

Published by
F. A. Thorpe (Publishing)
Anstey, Leicestershire

Set by Words & Graphics Ltd.
Anstey, Leicestershire
Printed and bound in Great Britain by
T. J. International Ltd., Padstow, Cornwall

To Steen

I

1

All this happened quite a few years ago. My mother had been unwell for some time. To put a stop to my brothers' nagging and my father's especially, she finally went to see the doctor she always saw, the doctor my family had used since the dawn of time. He must have been ancient at that point for I cannot recall ever *not* visiting him, nor can I recall him ever being young. I used him myself even though I now lived a good distance away.

After a brief check-up, this old family doctor swiftly referred her to Aker Hospital for further examination. Having been for several, no doubt painful, tests in rooms painted white, painted apple green, at the big hospital near the Sinsen junction on the side of Oslo I always like to think of as *our* side, the east side that is, she was told to go home and wait two weeks for the results. When they finally arrived, three weeks later rather than two, it turned out that she had stomach cancer. Her first reaction was as follows: Good Lord, here I've been lying awake night after night, year after year, especially when the children were small, terrified of dying from lung cancer, and then I get cancer of the stomach. What a waste of time!

My mother was like that. And she was a smoker, just as I have been my entire adult life. I know well those night-time moments when you lie in bed staring into the dark, with dry, aching eyes feeling life like ashes in your mouth, even though I have probably worried more about my own life than leaving my children fatherless.

For a while she just sat at the kitchen table with the envelope in her hand, staring out of the window at the same lawn, the same white painted fence, the same clothes lines and the same row of identical grey houses she had been looking at for so many years, and she realised she did not like it here at all. She did not like all the rock in this country, did not like the spruce forests or the high plains, did not like the mountains. She could not see the mountains, but she knew they were everywhere out there leaving their mark, every single day, on the people who lived in Norway.

She stood up, went out into the hallway, made a call, replaced the receiver after a brief conversation and returned to the kitchen table to wait for my father. My father was retired and had been for some years, but she was fourteen years younger than him and still working; though today was her day off.

My father was out, he always had something he needed to see to, errands to run my mother was rarely told about, the results of which she never saw, but whatever conflicts there had been between them were settled long ago. There was a truce now. As long as he did not try to run her life, he was left in peace to run his own. She had even started to defend and protect him. If I uttered a word of criticism or took her side in a misguided attempt to support the women's liberation, I was told to mind my own business. It is easy for you to criticise, she would say, who have had it all handed to you on a silver plate. You squirt.

As if my own life were plain sailing. I was heading full speed for a divorce. It was my first; I thought it was the end of the world. There were days I could not move from the kitchen to the bathroom without falling to my knees at least once before I could pull myself together and walk on.

★ ★ ★

When finally my father returned from whatever project he thought was the most urgent, something at Vålerenga no doubt, which was the place he was born, where I too

5

had been born seven years after the end of the war, a place he often returned to, to meet up with men his own age and background, to see *the old boys*, as they called themselves, my mother was still sitting at the kitchen table. She was smoking a cigarette, a Salem, I guess, or perhaps a Cooly. If you were scared of lung cancer you ended up smoking menthols.

My father stood in the doorway with a well-worn bag in his hand, not unlike the one I used in years six and seven at school, we all carried a bag like that then, and for all I know it was the same one. In that case the bag was more than twenty-five years old.

'I'm leaving today,' my mother said.

'Where to?' my father said.

'Home.'

'Home,' he said. 'Today? Shouldn't we talk about it first? Don't I get a chance to think about it?'

'There's nothing to discuss,' my mother said. 'I've booked my ticket. I've just had a letter from Aker Hospital. I've got cancer.'

'You have cancer?'

'Yes. I've got stomach cancer. So now I have to go home for a bit.'

She still referred to Denmark as *home* when she spoke about the town she came from, in the far north of that small country, even though she had lived in Norway, in Oslo, for forty years exactly.

'But, do you want to go alone?' he said.

'Yes,' my mother said. 'That's what I want.'

And when she said it like this she knew my father would be hurt and upset, and that gave her no pleasure at all, on the contrary, he deserves better, she thought, after so much life, but she did not feel she had a choice. She had to go on her own.

'I probably won't stay very long,' she said. 'Just a few days, and then I'll be back. I have to go into hospital. I may need an operation. At least I hope so. In any case I'm catching the evening ferry.'

She looked at her watch.

'And that's in three hours. I'd best go upstairs and pack my things.'

They lived in a terraced house with a kitchen and a living room on the ground floor and three small bedrooms and a tiny bathroom on the first. I grew up in that house. I knew every crinkle in the wallpaper, every crack in the floorboards, every terrifying corner in the cellar. It was cheap housing. If you kicked the wall hard enough, your foot would crash into your neighbour's living room.

She stubbed out the cigarette in the ashtray and stood up. My father had not moved, he was still standing in the doorway with the bag in one hand, the other insecurely raised in her direction. He had never been a champ when it came to physical contact, not outside the boxing ring, and frankly, it was not her strong point either, but now she pushed my father aside, carefully, almost lovingly so that she could get past. And he let her do it, but with so much reluctance, both firm and slow, it was enough for her to understand he wanted to give her something tangible, a sign, without putting it into words. But it's too late for that, she told herself, far too late, she said, but he could not hear her. Yet she allowed my father to hold her up long enough for him to understand there was enough between them after forty years together and four sons, even though one of them had already died, for them to live in the same house still, in the same flat, and wait for each other and not just run off when something important had happened.

★ ★ ★

The ferry she was travelling on, which we all travelled on when we headed south, was called the *Holger Danske*. Later she was docked and turned into a shelter for refugees, in Stockholm first, I've found out, and then in Malmö, and was now stripped down to scrap metal on some beach in Asia, in India or Bangladesh, but in the days I am talking about here, she still sailed between Oslo and this town in the far north of Jutland, the very town my mother grew up in.

She liked that boat and thought its poor reputation was unfair; *Not a Chanske*, as she was popularly known, but it was a much better ship, she thought, than the floating casinos which sail the route today, where the opportunities for drinking yourself senseless have become senselessly many and even though the *Holger Danske* might have rolled a bit from side to side when the weather was bad, that did not mean she was about to go down the great drain. I have thrown up on board the *Holger Danske* myself and never gave it a thought.

My mother was fond of the crew. With time she had made friends with many of them, for it was a small ship, and they knew who *she* was and greeted her as one of their own when she came up the gangway.

Perhaps on this occasion they noticed a new gravity in her manner, in her walk, in the way she looked around her, as she often would with a smile on her lips that was *not* a smile as there was nothing to smile about that anyone could see, but it was how she looked when her mind was somewhere else and definitely not in a place that those around her could have guessed. I thought she looked especially pretty then. Her skin was smooth and her eyes took on a strange, clear shine. As a small boy I often sat watching her when she was not aware I was in the room or perhaps had forgotten I was there, and that could make me feel lonely and abandoned. But it was exciting, too, for she looked like a woman in a film on TV, like Greta Garbo in *Queen Christina* lost in thought at the ship's bow close to the end of the film on her way to some other more spiritual place, and yet somehow she had managed to enter our kitchen and stop there for a while to sit on one of the red kitchen chairs with a smoking cigarette between her fingers and a so far untouched and unsolved crossword open in front of her on the table. Or she might look like Ingrid Bergman in *Casablanca* as she had the same hairstyle and the same curve along her cheek, but my mother would never have said: *You have to think for both of us* to Humphrey Bogart. Not to anyone.

If the crew of the *Holger Danske* had picked up on this or any other change in her way of greeting them when she crossed the gangway with her small brown suitcase of imitation leather, which is mine now and I still use wherever I go, there was no remark to that effect and I think she was grateful for that.

* * *

When she had found her cabin, she placed the suitcase on a chair, took a glass from the shelf above the sink, cleaned it carefully before she opened the suitcase and pulled out a half-bottle from underneath her clothes. It was Upper Ten, her favourite brand of whisky when she drank the hard liquor, which she did, I think, more often than we were aware of. Not that it was any of our business, but my brothers considered Upper Ten to be cheap shit, at least when you had access to duty free goods. They preferred malt whisky, Glenfiddich, or Chivas Regal which was sold on the ferry to Denmark, and they would hold forth at length about the distinctive caress of the single malt on your palate and other such nonsense, and we mocked my mother for her poor taste. Then she would give us an icy stare and say:

'And you are *my* sons? Snobs?'

And she would say: 'If you want to sin, it better sting.' And the truth is that I agreed with her, and to be honest I, too, bought the Norwegian label Upper Ten the few times I mustered the courage to go to the wine monopoly, and Upper Ten was neither single malt nor mild on your palate; on the contrary, it made your throat burn and the tears well up in your eyes unless you were prepared for the first mouthful. This is not to say that it was *bad* whisky, only that it was cheap.

My mother twisted the top off the bottle with a sudden movement and she filled the glass roughly three-quarters full, drained it in two gulps, and it burned her mouth and her throat so badly she had to cough, and then she cried a little too as she was already in pain. Then she put the bottle back under the clothes in her suitcase as if it were contraband she was carrying and the customs officers were at the door with their crowbars and handcuffs, and she washed her tears away in front of the mirror above the tap and dried her face and tugged at her clothes the way plump women nearly always do, before she went upstairs to the cafeteria which was a modest cafeteria in every sense of the word, and the menu was modest and manageable the way she liked it, and that made the *Holger Danske* the perfect boat.

She brought with her the book she was reading, and she was always reading, always had a book tucked into her bag, and if Günter Grass had published a novel recently, it was very likely the one she was carrying, in German. When I stopped reading books in German shortly after I left school for the simple reason I no longer had to, she dressed me down and told me I was intellectually lazy, and I defended myself and said I was not; it was a matter of principle, I said, because I hated the Nazis. That enraged her. She pointed a trembling index finger at my nose and said, what do you know about Germany and German history and what happened there? You squirt. She would often call me that. You squirt, she said, and it is true that I was not tall of stature, but then neither was she. But I was fit, I always have been, and the nickname 'squirt' implied both meanings: that I was fairly short of stature, like she was, and at the same time fit, like my father was, and that perhaps she liked me that way. At least I hoped she did. So when she dressed me down and called me a squirt, I was never in serious trouble. And I did not know that much about Germany at the time of this conversation. She had a point.

★ ★ ★

I cannot imagine she craved company in the cafeteria on board the *Holger Danske* and approached a table to engage someone in conversation, to find out what their thoughts were and what their dreams, for they were of her kind and had the same background, or the opposite, because they were different too, and it is in the way we differ that you find what is interesting, what is possible, she believed, and she searched for those differences and got a great deal out of them. On this occasion she sat down, alone, at a table for two and ate in silence and concentrated on her book over coffee after her meal, and when her cup was empty she tucked the book under her arm and stood up. The very moment her body left the chair, she felt so exhausted she thought she would collapse there and then and never stand up again. She clung to the edge of the table, the world drifted like the ferry did, and she had no idea how she would manage to get through the cafeteria, past the reception and down the stairs. And yet she did. She took a deep breath and walked with quiet determination between the tables, down the stairs to the cabins, and she had the expression on her face which I have already described, and only a few times did she lean against the wall for support before she found her cabin door, pulled the key from her coat pocket, and locked the door behind her. The minute she sat down on her bed, she poured a large measure of Upper Ten into her glass and downed it in three quick gulps, and she cried when it hurt.

2

After my mother had crossed the gangway of the *Holger Danske* and stepped on to the quay in the North Jutland town which was the town she grew up in and still referred to as home after forty years of fixed abode in Oslo, she walked along the harbourfront with the small brown suitcase in her hand and onwards past the shipyard which, in fact, had not been shut down, back then in the Eighties, when almost all other shipyards in Denmark collapsed like houses of cards. She walked past the old whitewashed gunpowder tower of Admiral Tordenskjold, which the town council had moved to the spot where it now stood from where it stood before, one hundred and fifty metres closer to the water. They had dug under the tower and laid down well worn railway sleepers, a giant winch was installed, and more than one thousand litres of soft soap were used to make the whole thing glide. And they did it. They dragged tons and tons of stone tower, centimetre by centimetre to its new location, which had been prepared in every possible way, so they could build a new dry dock for the shipyard without sacrificing one of the town's very few attractions. But it was a long time now since that operation had been carried out and she was really not quite sure if the story about the soft soap and the railway sleepers was entirely true; it did sound a bit odd, and she was not there when it happened. She was in Norway at the time, kidnapped by fate, like a hostage almost, but they did succeed. The tower had definitely been moved.

Three years earlier her father had been buried (irritable and impatient as he always had been) in the Fladstrand Church cemetery that bordered the lovely park, Plantagen, which shared with the cemetery its trees, shared its beech and ash and maple, in the same plot where her mother, wide eyed and confused, had lain down almost willingly two years before, where her brother had lain for thirty-five years, dazed and unwillingly after too short a life.

A dove was looking down from atop the family gravestone. It was made from metal so it could not fly away, but sometimes it went missing all the same and only a spike would remain. Someone had taken that dove, someone out there maybe had an entire collection of doves and angels and other small, Christian bronze sculptures in a cupboard at home and on long evenings

17

would close the curtains and take them out and run his fingers gently over the smooth, cold bodies. Every time someone nicked the dove, she had to order a new one from the undertakers just up the road and ask them to put it back. Maybe they did not do a very good job. The dove had gone missing three times in three years.

When she visited the cemetery these days, she could no longer leave it as she used to and walk or cycle past the care home to a flat in the centre of the town with an outside toilet, in a street which ran from the high street to the harbour, Lodsgade, it was called, and point to the windows, to the potted plants on the first floor, and say that this was where she had belonged, this was where she had become the person she was and then point to the window in the small room on the ground floor next to her mother's dairy shop, and try to say something about who her brother had been, and fail. Nor could she drop by in the early morning and knock on the door behind the open cast iron gate with fresh rolls in a paper bag, having just arrived on the ferry from Norway. No one would open that door. It was no longer her street. So she did not walk up Lodsgade and into town, instead she walked along the harbour with a strange flickering sensation in her chest, still

18

there after three years, and right up to the new railway station where she hailed a taxi. It signalled and pulled away from the kerb in the direction of Nordre Strandvej and drove past the nautical school and Tordenskjold's Redoubt, concealed behind its neatly manicured ramparts and cannons, behind the tall poplars along the road, and then past the rowing club. They had a cafeteria there, and she often sat at a table with a Carlsberg by the glass wall facing the small harbour and the sea, looking out at the little blue and red boats chugging in through the narrow entrance in the breakwater, to dock or to go back out again with fishing tackle on board, but then only as a hobby, as all serious fishing along this coast had died out several years ago.

The taxi drove on across the windswept open stretch of marram grass and sand and scrub, which the wind kept down at knee height one year after the other, and the sea lay taut this early morning like a blue-grey porous skin and the sky above the sea was as white as milk. Where the tarmac turned into gravel, the car pulled in between the ancient dog roses and gnarled pine trees and the whole trip lasted no more than a quarter of an hour. It was odd, she thought, for it felt like driving in slow motion, the gentle mist outside the car window, the grey light across the water, and the island out there where the beams from the lighthouse still cast pale, lazy flashes, and the last rosehips still hung from the bushes, each of them glowing red, blue almost, like little Chinese lanterns. When she looked out the opposite window, her head turned slowly from one side to the other, she moistened her lips with her tongue, looked down at her hands and slowly moved her fingers, and her skin felt numb and stiff, and she smiled for no reason.

★ ★ ★

Before she let the taxi go back to town she arranged with the driver to be picked up early in the morning four days later. The driver was only too happy to oblige, he said, it would get him up on time and that was not always the case, he had to admit, as he liked a beer or five in the evening.

'I'll tip you enough for ten beers,' my mother said. 'As long as you're here on time. It's important,' she said, 'I have a plan, you see,' and she raised her finger to the driver in a threatening gesture, but the young man grinned and then my mother smiled too.

'I'll be on time,' he said.

He got back into the driver's seat after

helping her up past the bushy pine tree to the terrace where he set down her suitcase and said: 'See you soon then,' and he backed the car in a semicircle before he drove across the lawn in front of the summer house where he had accepted his payment and a substantial tip, and he waved to her from behind the window and drove back into town with the light on the roof switched on through what could still be called the grey of dawn on a Thursday morning, early in November.

II

3

I did not realise that my mother had left. There was too much going on in my own life. We had not spoken for a month, or even longer, which I guess was not that unusual, in 1989, considering the things that happened back then, but it *felt* unusual. It felt unusual because it was intentional on my part. I was trying to avoid her, and I did so for I had no wish to hear what she might say about my life.

* * *

That afternoon when my mother took the Underground alone from Veitvet in Groruddalen down to Jernbanetorget with the brown suitcase in her hand to cross the damp square on the seaward side of the old Østbane Station, the headwind in her hair on her way to the flat, windswept terminal building that belonged to J.C. Hagen & Co., and the quay where the *Holger Danske* lay moored in what turned out to be her final week, I, at the same time came driving in a car that was not my own, from the gravel roads in Nittedal with my two daughters in the back, one ten years old, the other seven. The car was a 1984 silver-grey Volkswagen Passat that belonged to a man I had known for eight years, who would have given me his shirt, if I asked him for it.

It was starting to get dark, yes, the dark came rolling in like the tide used to do at the Jutland coast when I was as old as the girls were now, always surprisingly sudden, and it probably still does. It was early November, the girls in the back were singing a Beatles song they had learned from one of my old records, 'Michelle' it was, from *Rubber Soul*, and that song you would not call a masterpiece, but they liked Paul McCartney, he wrote songs that were easy for children to sing. And really, it sounded quite good, even the lines that were supposed to be in French sounded good, and I let go of the steering wheel as we drove the straight part of the road after Hellerudsletta towards Skjetten along the ridge and applauded as best I could.

It was good to have them both in the back seat. In that way they could talk to me about anything they wanted without having to look me in the eye, and I did not have to look *them* in the eye, and sometimes even they stopped looking at each other, and then the three of us would sit staring out of the windows in our separate directions without saying anything at all, while the car rolled along, and we all knew that things were not as they ought to be. The girls knew it, and I knew it, and she who was not in the car perhaps knew it best of all, and that was the reason she did not come with us on these trips.

This was the situation.

* * *

'Do you want to go fieldwatching?' I would sometimes shout from the hallway, and the girls nearly always replied:

'Yes!' from their two little bedrooms. 'Yes, we do!' and my wife would say:

'You just go. I'll stay here.'

And that was the whole point. That was what she was supposed to say. If she had said: 'Yes, I want to come,' then none of us would have known how a trip like that should be carried out, what to talk about, which roads to take.

So we went, the girls and I, down the stairs to the garage, through the yellow metal doors that slammed hard and hollow behind our backs, and most often we would go north to Nittedal, and sometimes to Nannestad, if there was time enough, and even all the way up to Eidsvoll and the river there, crossing the fine cast iron bridge while we stared into the water that flowed right below us and then park in the centre of that very place to eat waffles in a café we had been to before. But what we liked most of all were the gravel roads between the fields, the bumpy grey roads along the meadows and grainfields, going past the chequered sheep pens and the old electric fences with the white porcelain knobs on the posts, past the rusty, half-collapsed barbed wire fences. Just driving along those roads singing Beatles songs, uphill, downhill, on and on around the bends ahead, and the curves, the way it was that autumn, in 1989, in the fading light in Nittedal, at Nannestad and all the way up to Eidsvoll, the trees by the streams blown bare, and see it all arching up the colour of straw, in vast sheets and expanding rectangles, and around some bends see an orange colour come sneaking into view with a sickly glow where the stubble fields had been sprayed with Roundup only days ago, and then see them turn into the colour purple and after that an all-consuming black where the farmers had ploughed the fields just in time before winter came falling, and all light was drained out of them and simply vanished. We drove a little faster past those scary spots and laughed a bit too and cried out in high-pitched frightened voices:

'Watch out, for God's sake,' we screamed. 'Here comes a black hole!'

And I had explained to them about black holes, how things were sucked into them and were gone, how lives were sucked down, whole worlds sucked down, maybe *our* world sucked down, and I swerved the car to the opposite verge, and the girls squealed in the back and we had a narrow escape. And then we sighed with relief and laughed again, as we had never been this close to the cosmic abyss, and sang 'I Should Have Known Better' in harmony, while I hammered out the beat on the steering wheel.

And then the early dark descended and there was nothing more to see. Inside the car it grew dark around our shoulders and dark around our hands. Only the girls' hair was shining in the glow from the lights along the road, in red and in yellow, and the numbers glowed on the speedometer and the tiny blue light for the main beam went on and off with the oncoming traffic and we stopped our singing on the way past Skjetten and were silent on the bridge by the station at Strømmen.

Half a day might have passed since we left

the garage beneath our block of flats at home, and by now we were famished, our heads were swimming and felt numb around the edges, if you could say that a head has edges, but none of us wanted to break the silence inside the dark in the car where the indicator only ticked in green flashes to the right of the dashboard for a last detour along the edge of the forest, around the big hospital in a sharp curve before we turned in front of the old church and began the climb up the steep hill to the suburb where we lived, and I badly wanted to know what the girls were thinking about in the back. What *I* was thinking about was my divorce that came closer with each day, quietly swooping like an owl through the night, even though it was still just something we had agreed on, no date, no season set, we two who had held together for fifteen years and had these girls between us, with their shiny hair in red and in yellow, or to be honest, it was something she alone had agreed on. My face felt like a mask, my mouth was dry. If someone had asked me, how do you feel now? I would say, it hurts right here, and point to a place at the top of my chest, or rather at the very bottom of my throat. With each new morning, I left earlier for work. My eyelids stung when I sat on the bus. I did not know what I was facing.

Perhaps it might get even worse, later, when I was all alone? I was afraid it might get worse. I was afraid of what it would do to my body, the pain I felt in my chest, that would get worse, the struggle to swallow the tiniest bit of food, that would get worse, and the unexpected numbness in my legs, my thoughts swirling around like damaged radio waves, and in my sleep the wild, endless falls; all this would probably get worse, and then the shocking realisation that there was nothing I could do about it. No act of will would get me out of this state, no leap of thought pull me up. At times the only option was to sit in a chair and wait for the worst ravages to calm down so I could perform the most basic tasks: cut a slice of bread, go to the toilet, or drag myself all those exhausting metres through the hallway to lie down on my bed. More often than not I just gave up and slept where I sat and each time woke up with a start and a crackling blue light in my head when I heard her key in the door.

What I could manage were these drives through this landsape, Nittedal, Nannestad, Eidsvoll. There was something about the colours just before winter descended, or the lack of them, something about the lines along the forest's edge and the bends in the road; I thought I might remember it all, when things

31

were different. And there was the fact that I did not stand still, but on the contrary moved forward in my champagne-coloured Mazda, or as on this day, early in November 1989, in a silver-grey Volkswagen Passat that was not my own. There was something about the girls, as well, sitting in the back singing 'Eleanor Rigby' and 'When I'm Sixty-four', which were also written by Paul McCartney. I had never heard those songs sung this way before, and I thought that, too, was something I must never forget.

* * *

We came up the last hill in third gear, the road was long and steep and almost scary in winter when the ice lay shining in the wide curve, and then we drove along on the top in a semicircle around the blocks of flats past the trees, and finally turned towards one of them and drove into the garage where the automatic door was already open because it was wrecked and had been so for weeks. I stopped almost at the far end of the garage and backed into the space where the number of my flat was painted in yellow on the raw concrete wall where you could see the imprint of the rough boards right down to the annual rings, and the girls closed their eyes

32

tight shut, sucked the air down with a sharp sound and held it there, because this was a tight fit. On one occasion it went really wrong, and then there was a big fuss with a neighbour, who had now moved out, I am glad to say. He lived in the flat above ours, and on some evenings I would hear his stereo blast at full volume and his wife shouting, Turn it down, for God's sake.

This time it went without a hitch. I neatly slipped into my space with a good margin on both sides, and I praised my luck, as it was not my car, and we pulled ourselves out and slammed the doors hard, like we always did, to feel reckless, and the sound of it rolled down the long garage and came back again. I carefully checked that everything was according to regulations, the doors locked, the key in my pocket, before we walked up the stairs to the flat with me trailing reluctantly behind.

And then I entered the hall and walked into the kitchen, the living room, where everything was as it had been for almost ten years, the same posters on the walls, the same rugs on the floor, the same goddamn red armchairs, and yet not like that at all, not like it was in the beginning, when there were just the two of us against the world, just she and I, shoulder to shoulder, hand in hand, *there is just you and me*, we said to each other, *just you and me,* we said. But something had happened, nothing hung together any more, all things had spaces, had distances between them, like satellites, attracted to and pushed away at the same instant, and it would take immense willpower to cross those spaces, those distances, much more than I had available, much more than I had the courage to use. And nothing was like it had been inside the car either, driving through three or four districts in Romerike, in eastern Norway, east of Oslo. There the car was wrapped around me, but up here, in the flat, things fell out of focus and spun off to all sides. It was like a virus on the balance nerve. I closed my eyes to true up the world, and then I heard the bathroom door open and her footsteps across the floor. I would have known them anywhere on earth, on any surface, and she stopped right in front of me. I could hear her breath, but not close enough to feel it on my face. She waited. I waited. In one of the bedrooms the girls were laughing out loud. There was something about her breath. It was never like that before. I kept my eyes closed, I squeezed them tightly shut. And then I heard her sigh.

'For Christ's sake, Arvid,' she said. 'Please stop that. It's so childish.'

But I did not want to open my eyes. It was

all so clear to see. She did not like me any more. She did not want me.

'Your brother called,' she said. 'I think it was important.'

She stood there for a moment, then she turned and went back into the bathroom. I slowly opened my eyes and watched her back disappear. I rubbed the top of my chest with my hand.

4

When one of my brothers told me that my mother had gone straight to Denmark the moment she learned that she was ill, that they had not managed to speak to her in earnest before she left, to talk to her properly, to offer her the appropriate words of comfort, I made a quick decision and a quick telephone call, and precisely two days after her arrival, I, too, reached the North Jutland port early in the morning on the old and unfairly maligned ferry, the *Holger Danske*. I had overslept, I had missed breakfast in the cafeteria and a woman was standing outside banging the door to my cabin.

'We've docked,' she shouted, 'we've docked already! Get yourself up!' she shouted, and banged the door, and for a moment I wondered if she was one of those women I had made friends with in the bar the night before.

★ ★ ★

The small bar had been jam-packed when yesterday evening was slowly sliding into

36

damp night, and most of them were men in that bar, but a few women were there too, though not so many as there would have been today, and I had talked at length with several of them. I thought they were pretty.

It was a tight squeeze for anyone wanting to drink. Those of us who badly wanted to were crammed together as we carefully held our cigarettes between the fingers of one hand while holding a beer or a double whisky tight to our chest with the other, manoeuvring the glass very slowly up past the shirt collar and chin to swallow every precious drop.

There was a man there I did not like. I did not like his face when he looked at me. It was as if he knew something about my person that I myself was not aware of, which for him was clear as day, as if I were standing there naked, with no control over what he saw, nor could I see in his eyes what he saw in mine. But what he saw and what he *knew* made him feel superior to me and, in some strange way, I felt he had a right to. It could not be true, I had never seen him before, I was certain of that, he didn't know anything about my life. But his gaze seemed all-knowing and patronising each time he turned in my direction and he often did. It made me uneasy, I could not concentrate, and once when he shoved past me on his way to the gents or perhaps down to his cabin to fetch something he might have left down there, he barged into my shoulder in a way I found provocative. Some of the beer in my glass sloshed over the shirt I had bought only days before and considered pretty smart. I was convinced he had bumped into me on purpose and it made me feel threatened. In fact I feared for my life, I don't know why, but I got scared. I put down my beer on the bar and left.

First I made for the deck to clear my head, and it was dark there along the railing when I pushed open the heavy door and stepped outside. Lifeboats were hanging like Zeppelins above me in the vanishing light from the corridor I had left, and behind me the door slammed shut with an ominous bang. I could hear the sound of the sea and the wind sweeping along the ferry as she made her way through the waves. They were not tall, but nor was it calm; it was November and cold. The *Holger Danske* listed gently from side to side in the black night, where only the white spume on the crests of the waves near to the ship could be seen and the glow of my cigarette. It tasted vile. I thought maybe I was going to throw up, but the power of the sea was not stronger than my body could handle so I flicked the cigarette across the railing, out into the wind, and it hit the hull, and burst into sparks before it was lost in the dark. I stepped carefully back until I felt the cold wall touch my shoulder and I leaned against it and stood there staring until my eyes got used to the dark. I felt better. We had passed Færder Lighthouse, there was open sea to both sides, and the sea, it was like an old friend, and then it suddenly struck me that the man from the bar might come out here, and if he did, I was done for. He was bigger than me and could easily have thrown me overboard if he felt like it and then I would be gone for ever and no one would know exactly where. The thought grew so powerful I had to leave the deck though many times I have stood like that in the night, looking out over the sea: there is a calm there to be found which at times I have badly needed.

With some effort I managed to open the heavy door that the wind pushed hard against its frame, and I walked along the corridor and down the stairs to my cabin.

I had barely sat down on the bed to take off my shoes when there was a loud knock on the door. For a moment there, I literally froze with fear. I slowly stood up. I didn't know what to do. I stood listening and there was a second knock, a sharp, dry sound, and then I

39

suddenly knew exactly what to do. I clenched my right fist hard and walked the few steps to the door, tore it open and lashed out. The corridor was dim, and I could not see his face, in fact I could not see a damn thing, but I hit him on the jaw, right below the ear, I could feel it on my hand and he crashed into the opposite wall. More from the shock than the force of my blow, I guessed. But as I slammed the door shut and quickly double-locked it, I felt a stinging pain in my knuckles. I stood there, listening, holding my breath, but there was no sound from the corridor, and I stood there a bit longer, but it was still quiet, and I lay down on my bed and kept listening until I could not stay awake any longer and I fell asleep and in the early morning a woman was banging on my door:

'We've docked, we've docked already! Get yourself up!' And it seemed as if what had happened only a few hours earlier had taken place in a dream I was already starting to forget. But my hand was still sore and I could barely open it or clench it.

* * *

Now I was walking across the quay, shivering a little in the wind. I felt sick. I felt dizzy. I had my old reefer jacket on and a bag, that looked like a sailor's bag, slung over my shoulder and I walked up the winding Lodsgade, with all its memories, past Bar Sinatra, which was called the Ferry Inn when I was little.

I stopped outside the window of a small off-licence right next to what used to be the Palace Theatre on the long Danmarksgade. I often went to the Palace when I was a boy, my mother and I watched *Mutiny on the Bounty* there, with Marlon Brando starring as Fletcher Christian. She was a big fan of Brando, his sulky acting style, inarticulate and yet so clear, and she also loved the young Paul Newman in *The Hustler*, they both had something extra, some explosive quality, she said, whereas James Dean was all right. She did not really like James Dean, he was too whiny, too immature, he was spineless, she thought, and would quickly be forgotten. Montgomery Clift was undeniably the greatest; in *From Here to Eternity*, in *The Misfits*: his vulnerability, his eyes, his dignity.

The off-licence had not opened yet and I really had no need for the goods on its shelves, not after my night on the ferry, but I glanced at it anyway and then the sight of three bottles on display in the window made me stop, three different bottles containing the French spirit, Calvados, of three different qualities then, I assumed, and it suddenly occurred to me that I had never tasted Calvados. I decided that I could afford to buy the middle one, which would be good enough for me, if I *walked* to the summer house rather than take a taxi as I had intended to. I did have a car of my own, but just now it was in a garage in Norway with a broken drive shaft, and for all I knew it had already been repaired, but I had not got around to picking it up yet. So, at home, I walked or took the bus whenever I needed to go somewhere. That suited me well, for I could sleep on the bus, and I did. A lot. I slept as much as I could. There was nothing I liked better. But I was here now, and I really wanted one of those bottles of Calvados, and then I would have to walk. That's the way I am.

I did not feel like walking, I was tired, I could not remember the last time I was that tired, I was so tired it almost felt good and I weighed up the pros and cons and waited ten minutes for the shop to open its door, and went inside to buy the bottle in the middle and it was handed to me in a brown paper bag. A bit like they do in the movies, I thought, because I am Norwegian and in Norway we never get our liquor in brown paper bags and I liked the feeling of being in a film. I could be a man in a film. The walk to the summer house would be easier, if I was a man in a film.

* * *

Years before we had talked at length about Calvados, my mother and I, when she had urged me to read *Arch of Triumph* by Erich Maria Remarque.

'It's a good book,' she said, 'a bit sentimental perhaps, but you're the right age for it,' she said, and I was still not twenty and did not even take offence because I was not entirely sure what sentimental meant, not really, and did not realise that perhaps it was a slighting remark to make; that something was sentimental yet at the same time right for a young man not yet twenty. But that was not what she meant at all, it was not how she thought of me, she was merely stating the fact that I might benefit from reading it, and I did, too, benefit from that book, it was bull's eye, young as I was. We said to each other, my mother and I, wouldn't it be great one day to taste this liquor; a liquid that for me turned into the true magic potion, a golden nectar flowing through Remarque's novel and on in multiple streams, acquiring a strange, powerful significance and that, of course, because it was unobtainable, because they only sold one

43

single brand at the state monopoly and it was way beyond my means. But in *Arch of Triumph* they were forever ordering Calvados, Boris and Ravic, the two friends in the book who were refugees from Stalin and Hitler respectively, in Paris in the years before the German occupation, and it was Armageddon then, on all fronts, both back and forth in time, and the conversations they had about life left the same bitter taste in my mouth as singing the hymn, which goes: *Thank you for memories, thank you for hope, thank you Oh Lord for the bitter gift of pain*, which in fact I did at a funeral not long ago. Sing that hymn.

And so I walked up Danmarksgade in the half-light, the bottle tucked under my arm so the brown paper bag could be seen by all, and I was a man who had just bought this bottle of French alcohol very early in the morning, as soon as the shops had opened their doors, a man to be found in the movies only, and in certain books, mostly older books, written at the time of the Second World War, or just before, where the action was bound to a time that was long gone, and yet here I came walking, right there and then, adrift in time and space.

★ ★ ★

When I got to the summer house, I walked across the lawn, past the shed under the heavy dark pine branches with my bag over my shoulder and the bottle tucked under my arm, but my mother was not in the summer house though the door was unlocked. In fact she never locked it, not while she was there, not until she went back to Norway, and then she would turn everything off anyway, the water and electricity; my father was the one who locked up. He was always locking things; suitcases, bicycles and doors, and then later he would search like a maniac for the key while the rest of us stood there impatiently, shuffling our feet and freezing our arses off, waiting to get inside, thinking, how typical, how bloody typical. 'You can never be too careful,' he would snap, his face blushing in the cold.

'There was a book on the table, not Günter Grass this time, but Somerset Maugham, in English, an old Penguin paperback of *The Razor's Edge*, about an American pilot who travelled to India after the First World War where he experienced a spiritual change, and that book had always annoyed me, it is a hippie book, I thought, or at least has turned into one, why the hell would she want to read that book now? I put my bag down and went back outside, still holding the bottle, and walked between the pine trees, along the gravel road to the end where the dog roses grew thick and left the road to follow the path through the marram grass to the beach. It was quite windy and I saw her at once. She was sitting on a low sand dune with her warm coat wrapped tightly around her and her collar turned up against the wind, and the wind whipped her dark curls, and I thought, she has not gone grey yet, at least not much, though she was now over sixty, and she sat there alone, her head held high like she always did in a way some found arrogant. But really she was just preoccupied and was staring dreamily across the sea, probably thinking about something quite different than what was in front of her while she smoked a cigarette; a Cooly I guessed, or a Salem, or, more likely, the cheaper Danish menthol brand, Look.

I am sure she heard me coming, but she did not turn around. When I was quite close to her, I called out softly:

'Hello!'

Still she did not turn around, merely said: 'Don't start talking right away.'

'It's me,' I said.

'I know who it is,' she said. 'I heard your thoughts clatter all the way down from the road. Are you broke?'

46

Jesus Christ, I knew she was ill, that she might even die; it was why I was here, it was why I had come after her, I was sure of it, and yet I said:

'Mother, I'm getting a divorce.'

And I may have seen it from her back, how she pulled herself together and shifted her weight from one place inside her body to another, from where *she* was, to where she thought maybe *I* was.

'Come here, sit down,' she said. And she moved to one side as if to make room for me, though there was plenty of it and she patted the wiry grass and said almost impatiently:

'Come on then!' and I walked up and sat down beside her on the ledge. I took the bottle from the brown paper bag and placed it between my feet, twisted it into the white, powdery sand, so it would not keel over, but I do not think she noticed. In fact, she did not even look at me, and that made me feel uncomfortable.

5

Many years before, in the early Seventies, I went to a college in the Dælenenga district of Oslo, on the corner of Dælenenggata and Gøteborggata. In order to get there I had an almost ridiculously short distance to walk every morning because I had a small flat right down the road from the college, at Carl Berners Plass. I had just turned twenty, it was the first place I lived which was not my childhood home: the terraced house in Veitvet where I grew up in the late Fifties and Sixties, and I had moved out as soon as I got my student loan. That was what you did back then, whether you wanted to or not, *if you were allowed to go further*, as it was still called, in our street, and in many other streets.

The first thing I did was to go into town and buy a stereo with some of the money, a TR 200 Tandberg amplifier, a Lenco record player and a couple of 20 watt loudspeakers of a make I can no longer recall, but the sound was superb, and to be honest the whole thing was identical to the stereo my eldest brother had put together and bought with *his* student loan. I was going through a phase where I copied him a lot. Not in everything, of course. I was a Communist in those days, a Maoist, which he was not; but he was so talented with his hands, with carpentry, drawing and painting, that it did not even occur to me to try and emulate him. Instead I read books. Many books, and I guess to him it looked so intriguing and intense, the way I lost myself in those books, that sometimes he tried to copy *me*, and that made me happy.

★　★　★

If I walked from the college at the corner and down Gøteborggata, which I often did, I soon reached the Freia chocolate factory. My mother worked there. She stood at the assembly line in Confectionery eight hours a day, five days a week, plus overtime and had done so for many years. All over Dælenenga and Rodeløkka there was a smell of chocolate, of cocoa, in the mornings especially, when the air was sharp and a little damp maybe, and it was only when I had been out drinking too many pints the night before that I found the smell unpleasant. Otherwise there was a feeling of comfort about it that brought back to me certain days in my childhood, with certain faces attached and family gatherings with tables laid and tablecloths and the slanting sun through gleaming white blinds and then me, in the middle of it all with this sudden feeling that everything around me was so fine, so perfect. Sometimes, in the late nights, in my small flat at Carl Berners Plass, in Dælenenga, I allowed that feeling to well up from the past, and then I would long for my childhood with such teeth grinding intensity that I almost frightened myself.

When classes were over or I was just fed up sitting in the canteen, I would often stroll down Gøteborggata and turn right towards Dælenenga Stadium where the workers' entrance to Freia was, and I would stop and lean against the brick wall surrounding the factory and they smelled good those bricks, they smelled of nature, smelled of places I had been with my father, the forests of Østmarka, Lillomarka, and I gaped up at Arnold Haukeland's heavy, shiny, slowly rotating metal sculpture on a plinth near the entrance. It had been there only two or three years at the time, and was supposed to be a wind harp, and sounds were meant to fold out from it when the wind blew, like music, I had been told, but no music had ever been heard as far as I knew. I smoked the Petterøe 3 cigarette I had rolled myself, and I had all the time in the world in a way I have never had since. I stood in the sunshine and waited for my mother who would soon come from the huge building and walk along the flagstoned path to the gate when her shift was over. I could see her from afar when she came through the door, and every time she did, I found myself thinking of Rudolf Nilsen's poem which begins:

Long had I seen you as you came
for always did I know when you were
    near,

which, strictly speaking, was a poem to his girlfriend some time back in the Twenties. But I thought about it because of where I was, right between Dælenenga and Rodeløkka and Grünerløkka on the eastern side of central Oslo which, after all, was Rudolf Nilsen's territory, just outside a factory where many of the girls he knew had probably worked, and even if it was my mother who was walking towards the gate and not my fiancée, then surely she was near to me, as it says in the poem; it felt that way.

I straightened up, left the wall to support itself and called out:

'Freia chocolate!'

'Not for me,' she called.

'Freia toffee?'

'Not bloody likely,' she said, blushing because the security guard was listening and laughing at us.

'So, what are *you* doing here?' she said in a hushed voice when she reached the gate and the guard had let her out. 'Are you broke?' she said.

Of course I was. I always was, but I said:

'What? Are you insinuating that I've been standing here waiting for my mother who is coming from the factory exhausted after a hard day's work just because I happen to be a bit broke and then hope that she might spare me some change. Honestly, Mother.'

'How much do you need?' she said.

I shrugged.

'Look here,' she said and stuck her hand into her small handbag, found her worn brown purse which she opened in a furtive manner that was studied and practised over many years to prevent inspection from a nosy husband who no longer had the economic power in the family, and she deftly eased out a hundred kroner note she had folded into a tiny chip which she pressed into my seemingly reluctant palm.

'Take it,' she said.

I saw at once what kind of note it was. 'Jesus Christ, Mother, a hundred kroner. That's too much.'

And in fact it was. In comparison, my rent was 170 kroner a month.

'And we'll say no more about it,' she said. 'Not a word to your father, either.'

'Him I never see,' I said.

'That's not entirely his fault, is it?' my mother said, and she was right about that, and it was fine, I would not tell him anything, why would I? And there was no doubt the money came in handy. But the reason I was there that day was not just the fact that I was broke, not at all, being broke was a way of life, I hardly noticed it any more. I was there because I had something to tell her, something she could not have known and would never have guessed.

'Why don't we have a coffee before you go home?' I said. 'At Bergersen's?' And it was such an unusual suggestion that she said yes without thinking twice. What we normally did was walk together up Gøteborggata, along Dælenenggata to Carl Berners Plass, past the Ringen Cinema, where I watched *Zorro's Fighting Legion* in two parts when I was eleven, on two Saturdays with an unbearably long week in between, and then we would cross the junction and walk up Grenseveien

53

to the Underground station while we talked
about books we had read, new films we had
seen and old films we had seen again, such as
Saturday Night and Sunday Morning with
the young Albert Finney in the lead, which
that very week had been on TV. My mother
liked him a lot too, Albert Finney, when he
stood there at his lathe in the bicycle factory
right at the start of the film with his shirt
sleeves rolled up and bluntly declaimed what
he thought of the older workers and the way
they were stuck in the mud of the pre-war
years and all the things he definitely was *not*
going to waste his life on, and there was no
bloody way that he would ever allow himself
to be kept down like *they* had been:

*'I'd like to see anybody try to grind me
down, that'll be the day. What I'm out for is
to have a good time, all the rest is
propaganda!'* he said through tight lips and,
of course, that was so much childish
nonsense, my mother knew that better than
anyone. Yet she waved her glowing cigarette
and like Albert Finney in the factory
concourse she said: *'All the rest is propaganda!'* in a rather loud voice right there on
Carl Berners Plass, with narrow eyes and
rolling Nottinghamshire 'r's and a sudden
dark laughter that made me a bit anxious,
though I, too, thought it was a cool thing to

say. Then we changed the subject and started talking about the foreman in Confectionery who took liberties with the female workers, and there were almost nothing *but* female workers at Freia, or at any rate in Confectionery. She couldn't stand him any longer, the slimy bastard, and was now planning a counter-attack, and she and I discussed how such a counter-attack might be carried out.

We were walking up to Bergersen's café, which in fact was not its name, I just called it Bergersen's because a man called Bergersen sat on a chair in the corner by the window every single day, reading the same newspaper. Look, there's Bergersen, the staff would say. The café was in a short street which ran diagonally behind the Ringen Cinema and was an extension of Tromsøgata, and bore the same name, but here it turned into a blind alley, an almost anonymous place.

Once inside we ordered two coffees and Napoleon cakes, and took off our coats and hung them on the coat stand by the entrance, and I was already away, explaining to her what was happening in my life, that I had decided to stop attending the college at the corner of Dælenenggata and Gøteborggata where I had been a student for two years with my student loans and stereo and late nights with pints of beer and everything that went with it, because the Communist Party I was a member of had launched a campaign to persuade as many of its members as possible to become industrial workers. Not by force or anything, but a man from the central committee had come to my small flat and had spoken passionately for a good while and explained how the new Great War would soon be upon us, maybe even early in the New Year when you considered how the Soviet Union was arming herself, surely that was something I had realised after this year's summer camp on Håøya? And then it made no sense, did it, to remain where I was right now, surely we all wanted to be with the boys, didn't we, where *they* were? That was the expression he used, *the boys*, and by *the boys* he meant the industrial workers, and he pointed with conviction out of the window, into the world, but in fact in the wrong direction, for he was not pointing to where my mother laboured only a few blocks away as an industrial worker, and was one of the boys, so to speak, even though the majority were women in that factory, nor did he point to where my father worked as an industrial worker and was one of the boys only a few stops away on the Underground. What he pointed at was the Munch Museum at the end of Finnmarkgata.

I often went to the Munch Museum on Sundays to stand before the colourful, soft yet sinister paintings I loved so much, and I really didn't want to disappoint anyone, that's the way I have always been. So it was easy to tell where this was heading.

Only a week after that conversation I attended a meeting at the college along with the other students who shared my view of the world and of politics, and *I* was the one who gave the talk about how important it was for the party to grow deep roots in the working class in times such as these. It was a fairly good talk, but I could not shake off the feeling that the working class I spoke of was not quite the same as the one my mother and father belonged to on a daily basis. They resembled each other, it was true, but they had different qualities and, strictly speaking, belonged to separate worlds. This made me a little uncomfortable, but I must have been the only one who noticed, because when I had finished they all slapped me on the back and said it was a damned fine speech and how interesting it had been to listen to it, and I do not know which houses and streets they grew up in, the other students who attended the meeting, but when it was over, I was the only one to declare I would give up my place at college. And that I did. It was the same as when I was a Boy Scout. I was the only one in the Roe Deer Patrol who took the Scout's oath seriously. In many ways it was the same.

All this I tried to tell my mother. I had hung my coat on the coat stand, I could see the lady from behind the counter on her way towards us with our coffees and Napoleon cakes on a tray and as I turned in my chair to sit face to face with my mother during this moment we had to ourselves, and the words still flowing from my mouth, I suddenly saw the flat of her hand come sweeping across the table like a shadow, and hit me on the cheek, and the sound it made was the loudest sound in the room. Outside the window was a man unloading crates of flowers from his van for the shop next door, the sun touched the brick wall of an apartment building across the street. Two girls came cycling on their way home from school with their bags on the pannier, they were no more than ten years old and looked a bit cold in their flimsy dresses, and deep inside I felt the old yearning for a sister, and if I had had a sister, my life would have been different, and I would not have been the person sitting here, at this moment, at Bergersen's café. But of course I had only brothers, three even, and my cheek stung, I could feel it turn red and hot, and I did not know what to do or say. I stared down at the table, I stared at the counter; from the corner of my eye I saw my mother stand up from her chair. The room was completely silent, only the hum from the soft-ice machine could be heard, and the lady with the tray froze halfway to our table before she came all the way over, carefully put down the tray and vanished, and then I remembered the hundred kroner note. I put my hand in my pocket and pulled out the well-folded note.

'Here,' I said. 'I guess you want this back.' I felt the other cheek beginning to glow. I looked up. She stood with her coat over her arm, her face was pale and her eyes were moist.

'You idiot,' she said. And then she left.

★　★　★

I do not remember leaving the café, if I ate my Napoleon cake first or even ate them both, if I paid with the hundred kroner note, nor do I remember what I did during the next few days. But now I was sitting next to my mother on a sand dune by the coast in far north-eastern Denmark one early morning in November 1989 and remembered it all. Across the water was an island called Hirsholmen. On that island was a lighthouse I had seen every single summer of my entire life and my mother, too, had seen it *her* entire life, and I wondered how it might affect your way of thinking, if you always had a lighthouse in the corner of your eye.

She took the last drag of her cigarette and stubbed it out in the loose sand in front of her with a slow, somewhat heavy movement and turned towards me.

'What have you got there?' she said, pointing to the half-buried bottle between my feet.

'Calvados,' I said.

'Calvados,' she said, and then she nodded a little sleepily. '*Arch of Triumph*, then?'

'Yes,' I said. '*Arch of Triumph*.'

She nodded again, a little distant still, a little heavy: 'It's a fine book,' she said. 'A little sentimental, perhaps. You'd best be under twenty when you read it for the first time.'

'I guess you're right,' I said.

6

She thought she knew who I was, but she did not. Not on the beach that day in 1989, not in Bergersen's café nearly fifteen years earlier, not before I was a Communist. She did not pay attention, she turned her gaze to other things. She saw me come in and didn't know where I had been, she saw me go out and didn't know where I was heading, how adrift I was, how sixteen I was without her, how seventeen, how eighteen, how desperately walking along Trondhjemsveien I was, up and down Route E6 between Veitvet and Grorud. In both directions, first past the women's prison that lay gloomily to my right like a shadowy, secretive, improbable vacuum behind thick stone walls, before the low blocks on Kaldbakken appeared to the right and the tall blocks on Rødtvet to the left, rising up towards the woods that were so deep and so big that you could easily disappear in them and be lost for ever, if that was what you longed for.

And it was autumn when I walked, November, always November, late evenings with drizzling rain and the street lights flashing past high above my head and because

I walked so fast, it was as though they came on and off, those lights, never stopping and could suddenly crackle sharply in the damp air and send off flashes of blue lightning around them while my words were circling in my brain and my thoughts sparkling like an electric current and perhaps looking blue as light sometimes does, if you could slice through my brain to study up close what was happening in there.

★ ★ ★

My school was down on Østre Aker Vei, by Grorud railway station and the star shaped blocks, as they were known, where the railway workers lived; train drivers, ticket collectors, engineers, but before I got as far as that I turned right at the junction with Trondhjems-veien where the football club was and the grass pitch and on past the church and the cemetery and zigzagged downhill before making a final detour past Heimdal, the red building where the young Christians came together on evenings like this, where I had tried to pass through the eye of a needle, but was turned away, by myself, halfway up the stairs every single time because of my lack of faith. And in the windows the lamps were lit each time I passed by, and there were young bodies moving inside, boys' bodies like my own, but most of all girls with their girls' bodies that were Christian from head to toe, that managed to be Christian, in spite of their curves and lines along their hips and the round breasts under their blouses and their smooth Christian skin glowing with an ease that I had not been granted. I merely felt embarrassed when I thought of what they had done: laid their lives in hands that were not their own, but in the hands of what they thought was a higher power, and this power threw such a brilliant light they could bathe their souls in, and they sang of that light without blushing or shame, with their eyes upturned and blissful smiles on their lips. And they were having such a good time, running around laughing out loud and no matter what they were up to, their Christian faith would protect them.

But I no longer stopped on the stairs or outside the windows looking in, I was beyond that, I no longer wished to be inside, I held my life in my own hands. But it was not easy to be alone and to be honest, I could not bear it.

I walked on around the bend and down to my school where the buildings stood dark in the autumn evening and looked strange, alien even, in an almost menacing way. When I got there, I crossed the empty courtyard and the sound of my boots threw echoes off the walls on both sides and suddenly I could feel that my mother was there. I'm not joking, she really was and she looked at me through the damp dark in the yard of Groruddalen School, and the windows on both sides showed no sign of life at this time of night, no one leaning out of a first floor window to call something nice to me, something embracing I had longed to hear, and I knew what she was thinking: Has the boy enough about him, she thought, will he manage on his own or is he too fragile? I was convinced she believed I was too fragile, that there was something about my personality that made her sceptical, that my character had a flaw, a crack in the foundations only she knew about, things had been handed to me, was what she thought, but life was not like that, nor should it be.

7

When we came back to the summer house, we were both a little cold. I put the bottle on the table and went over to the Jøtul stove that my father had bought straight from the factory and fitted to the chimney that was already in place so my mother and father could keep the summer house warm to their hearts' content and then stay on in the summer house through the colder seasons.

There was firewood in the basket. I knelt down and built a fire with plenty of kindling and because the draw was good, I got it going at my first attempt. It was a fine stove; the heat spread around the room as the flames took hold behind the cast iron, and I grew sleepy when the heat hit my face. I closed my eyes.

'I'm getting a divorce,' I said.

'So you said,' she said. 'I wouldn't know why. Why you're getting a divorce.'

She was behind me somewhere. In the kitchen, perhaps. I stared into the stove. The fire was burning nicely now.

'It can't go on,' I said, and I could hear how it sounded like it was my idea, that it was my decision, but it was not.

'I suppose she's the one who wants the divorce,' my mother said.

'Why do you say that?'

'I know you,' she said.

'You don't know me,' I said, but she did not even bother to reply.

'You could have got divorced yourself,' I said.

'Oh, you think so. But I didn't.'

'If you know me so well, then why don't you know why I'm getting divorced?'

'Oh, Arvid,' she said, 'drop it.'

I opened my eyes. I was still kneeling in front of the stove. I stood slowly up and looked at her.

'I need to lie down for a bit,' I said. 'Half an hour or so, if that's all right with you?'

'That's quite all right,' my mother said. She had sat down by the table and lit a cigarette and her voice sounded strangely subdued, flat almost, like it was coming from behind a wall, and so I did not go into one of the two small bedrooms as I otherwise would have done, but instead I lay down on the old sofa, for I did not want to be alone while I slept and did not want her to be without me while she was awake.

At first the sofa swayed like the ferry only a few hours earlier, and it made me feel a little sick, but then I got used to it and after a while it was quite pleasant. The coarse cover of the sofa smelled of summer and the Sixties, I could hear my mother leafing through a book at the table behind me, *The Razor's Edge*, I supposed. And then I heard the tiny click of her lighter as she lit up another cigarette and I let go, went into freefall and was asleep before I hit the ground.

★ ★ ★

Before I was fully awake I knew I was not in my childhood home, nor in the flat where I lived, in a suburb I referred to as Eagles' Nest, and I was not lying in the bed where I normally slept and woke up and had been lying so many nights staring into the dark, but instead I was in this summer house, which had been such an important part of my life. This small plot had saved me from Hudøy island again and again when I was still at school. Hudøy was a holiday camp way out in the Oslo Fjord where they sent the children who had nowhere else to go for the summer when both parents had to work or they did not have the money to go anywhere at all, or for no other reason than for the children to feel the sun on their faces, the wind in their hair and the salt water on their bodies. It was the common cure for anything and everything that might ail a child in the Sixties, but I knew even then that I would not be able to bear the pressure of the other boys in the dormitory, the dining hall, during morning exercises: that I would pray like the others prayed, on my knees by the bed at night, if pray was the thing to do. I did what the others did because I lacked the strength to stand alone in the crowd with my fear and my freedom.

As I rose through the layers of sleep I heard voices, my mother's voice and a deep male voice I knew well and that was because its owner had never been able to keep the volume down no matter how hard he tried. The voice had a richness that regardless of which room it filled, made the walls rumble, the furniture even, and my chest rumbled as I lay on the sofa. But they were really trying their best to be quiet so as not to wake me, and I did not stir, but lay with my nose into the sofa cover and my hands folded at the back of my neck. I often woke up in this position back then, as if I had ducked for cover, or a weapon was pointed at my head, like in a news report from Africa, from Congo or Angola, or like I had seen in films from war, where the captured prisoners were lying like that, side by side, with their faces to the ground, dust in their nostrils, stripped of dignity, the scorching sun and the burning, cracked lips, the white smiles of the Allied soldiers and their white cigarettes.

I heard my mother say:

'What he's doing is absolutely necessary. It just couldn't go on like that, the situation was intolerable. But many are against him, the army is against him, it's all hanging by a thread. I don't know what will happen now.' And then she said: 'I hope to God I live long enough to see how it all turns out,' and she started to cry, and then she was silent and became furious instead. I could tell from the way she lit her cigarette, how she failed with her first, hectic attempts and the male voice said:

'Let's go over to my place and have some coffee and let the lad sleep. He looks like a calf on its way to the slaughterhouse.' His deep voice resonated through my bones.

'He's getting a divorce,' my mother said.

'I'll be damned,' said the man, whose surname was Hansen, and he was never called anything but Hansen.

Hansen was my mother's best friend even though the two of them spent most of their time in different countries, and I am certain that they never wrote to each other. Hansen

69

was a retired railway worker. He lived in town in a low redbrick tenement and rode a moped to his summer house as often as he could, no matter what time of year it was.

'I've never been divorced myself, so I really don't know much about it,' Hansen said, and a pause followed, and then I heard him say: 'What have you got there?'

'It's a bottle Arvid bought,' my mother said. 'It's Calvados, French spirit.'

'Well, the lad's all right for money then,' Hansen said. 'Come on, let's talk politics on my side of the hedge. I'll treat you to a cup of coffee and some cake too, if you are up for it,' and maybe he touched her cheek just then.

I heard them rise from the table and walk towards the door. They had been discussing Gorbachev, the man with the map of an unknown nation on his forehead, who was now leader of the Soviet Union, appointed to that post the year before, who would turn out to be the last leader of a state which was a seventy year long experiment where everything had gone to hell a long time ago. But no one realised that yet. That Gorbachev would be the last. Not even he.

My youngest brother had gone to the Soviet Embassy in Oslo and convinced the staff it was important to give him a photo of their president, even though the cult of personality was finally over and done with, even in China where it really took off for some years, it could not be denied, and my brother carefully carried the photo home and had it framed and gave it to my mother for her birthday.

'Hang that above your bed,' he said, 'then you can talk to him before you fall asleep. Like Arvid used to talk to Mao.'

And she did, for fun really, but it was not true that I used to speak to Mao. That would have been childish. I did have a picture of Mao above my sofa bed in the early Seventies, that is true, because that was the only place I had for it. But I had a picture of Bob Dylan there too and one of Joni Mitchell on a beach in California (*Oh California, California, I'm coming home*) and a reproduction of a landscape by Turner, the English painter, for I had read somewhere that he painted his pictures with brushes dipped in tinted steam, and I thought that was a beautiful way to put it, so when I came across this poster of one of his paintings of the sea from outside the town of Whitby on the English coast, a town I had been to the year before, I bought it because I was certain I could see that it was true.

The picture of Mao I had was the well-known retouched photograph where he

71

sits hunched over his desk writing with one of those Chinese brush pens, and I always thought, or hoped, that it was not one of his political or philosophical articles he was writing, but one of his poems, perhaps the one which begins:

Fragile images of departure, the village
    back then.
I curse the river of time; thirty-two
    years have passed.

for it showed the human Mao, someone I was drawn to, someone who had felt how time was battling his body, as I had felt it so often myself; how time without warning could catch up with me and run around beneath my skin like tiny electric shocks and I could not stop them, no matter how much I tried. And when they let up at last and everything fell quiet, I was already a different person than I had been before, and it sometimes made me despair.

But the Seventies were long gone. Only half a year before this November, I and a crowd of people I used to know back then, in the Seventies, had been standing side by side on the pavement opposite the Chinese Embassy in Oslo shouting slogans and protests and had delivered a letter to His Excellency the

Chinese Ambassador, and I do not recall if he himself or someone else came to the gate, or if anyone at all came out to receive the letter. Just the same, we pleaded urgently with the Chinese authorities, the Chinese Communist Party we had held in such high regard for so many years, to stop killing the students in the square they called Tiananmen, stop killing the young workers who had joined the students, we begged them to stop the stream of blood which in June 1989 flowed to every corner of the big square like the streams in a delta of red, and just as urgently, we called for democracy in China, and it felt strange to stand there shouting for democracy in the great country that had once been our Jerusalem, where the sun no longer rose in the east for anyone but those who lived there. Soon to be a billion strong. Mao had died nearly thirteen years earlier and thousands of us marched through the Oslo night with pictures on poles and black flags in the wind and black mourning bands around our arms and I remember thinking, what do we do now? But in June 1989 it just felt strange and a little sad. Many of those around me I had not seen for ten years and they all looked older, some with narrow stripes of grey at their temples, and there was nothing more we could do, and the air fell empty as it had been before we came, and I left the pavement opposite the Chinese Embassy with the woman who had been my life for fifteen years, but did not want me any more.

8

I found a job in a factory not far from Økern Station on the eastbound Underground line. I had worked there for two months now. I stood by a machine and watched the light spill into the hall in many slanted columns from the huge windows to the car park. In the grey dust the columns looked so compact that you could bang your head if you walked into them, and it was almost strange that no one did. I hoped the air was not so dense, so grey between the pallets at the assembly line where I stood, but of course it was, and denser still. It was from there the dust came.

In the evenings the windows were black. The slanted columns dissolved and vanished, and the light shifted from the windows to the air above the machines where fluorescent tubes hung suspended from the ceiling in long, furry chains, and the dust too shifted and whirled above our heads like glittering confetti.

★ ★ ★

Most days we worked the same shifts and stood together at the assembly line, we who formed what I called the A Team, which everyone called it now, but on other days we worked in a rota and there might only be the two of us on the platform along the machine working with other people from other shifts. I never got used to it. It was like coming home from holiday after two months away and my father had rearranged the living room, so everything was back to front, and for days I would turn from the hall and crash into a chair when my brothers and I came in to watch TV.

The workers from the other shift had no idea how to support each other like we did on the A Team; the rhythm would fall apart, and I was always more tired after days like that. Each time I rushed off to get the forklift to bring more pallets of paper I would then lower on to the lifts we used to save our backs, the supply of paper at my station would run out. Then the whole belt had to be stopped because the folded sheets with text and pictures were trapped on the chain and didn't fall into place like they should. Then the man we called Sony Amerika got incredibly angry and would scream at me and try to stare me down with his merciless look in a way that Hassan, the machine operator from the A Team would never have done. They had the same job, but never worked the same shift, and why the hell didn't Sony Amerika drive the forklift himself, why did I always have to do it? My job was to feed my station. I should have got furious, abandoned the machine and sat on a pallet rolling a cigarette with my back to Sony, but they would call it sabotage, and not one from that shift would have backed me, this I knew. So I did not do it, just gave him an evil and merciless stare in return.

* * *

On the production line, it was Elly I got on with best. We had the same rhythm, the same stops and starts and we caught each other's eye and laughed when, more than often, we moved in such harmony as if we were one person with four arms, and she would solve crossword puzzles and I would read books when our stations were full and everything was running smoothly. Then Hassan was happy and rested his legs on the chain guard and read magazines with porous pages and Arabic type. When I ran across the hall to get the forklift, Elly would move over and fill my station so the machine did not stop. No one else did that.

Every half-hour we swapped places. We filled five of the stations with bulky paper that whirled dust into our faces, but was kind to our hands and produced by Follum in Norway. In the last station we put shiny, stiff paper produced in Finland by Kirkniemi.

When we swapped stations, Elly nearly always bumped into me with a swing of her hip that pushed me head first into the pallets sending paper flying to all sides when I landed, and her round hip left its imprint on my thigh, and there it would stay, and she laughed, and I laughed and Hassan threw up his hands in despair.

At times, when I was fed up with him, and he was not there, I mimicked Sony Amerika's Deep South accent, an accent he would never get rid of, and many thought I was good at it. But I always felt bad about it a few hours later, after the early shift or the late shift or after overtime at night on my way down the hill between the factories towards the Økern Centre to catch the Underground home. My job was to make the workers unite, not divide them, that was the party line, and Sony Amerika was not the enemy.

★　★　★

I came off the night shift and stood waiting on the platform when the train on the opposite side arrived, stopped, let passengers off and let new ones in, it took a long time that, and then the train left. A stream of warmly dressed people in puffa jackets and dark coats, in short jackets of tweed, of wool, got off at this station, with scarves around their necks and gloves on their hands, or mittens, and they were all on their way to companies in the area. There were more of them here than at any other station in the valley.

When they had all gone up the steps, a girl came out from behind the shelter, I had seen her before. She must have got off the train that had just left and instead of floating with the crowd up the steps, through the barriers to the square outside, she had slipped behind the back of the shelter with its arched roof, like a Chinese pagoda, and was now standing at the edge of the platform waiting for the next train. She wiped her mouth with the blue sleeve of her jacket, or rather her coat, it looked a bit short on her, she looked a bit cold, she had a fringe and long blonde hair like Joni Mitchell on the cover of the album, *Blue*, but she was younger. And then my train arrived, the doors crashing open and I stepped in and went to the window in the opposite door and stood there watching her until we left. She saw me looking at her, and she turned away.

This happened several times when I was going home from the night shift; she would come out from behind the shelter and stand there in her blue jacket or coat with the too short sleeves and look frozen waiting for the next train and then turn away when she saw that I was looking at her.

This was something you could see in the early morning if you paid attention and did not allow yourself to be drowned in the noise around you, and even more when you were tired and exhausted and only able to concentrate on one thing at a time.

★ ★ ★

Then the train stopped at Carl Berners Plass, the blue station; Tøyen was green, Grønland was yellow, beige, almost, and so on in a system which was not a system, and it always annoyed me that it was not, for it would have been so good if there had been a system rather than everything being so hopelessly, half-heartedly Norwegian as it was now, but instead a bit European, a little bit continental, because, hey, here was a station of grey concrete for no apparent reason and it looked completely unfinished and raw with its rough damp walls, and would remain like this for ever because someone thought it artistic.

Anyway, I got off at Carl Berners Plass, the blue station. I was on my way home after a double shift, which meant overtime and good money. I was so tired I felt drunk. During the last few hours at the machine before the new shift was on we fooled about and laughed at the most feeble jokes and our heads were light as helium balloons. My body felt loose, like rubber, but in a way I enjoyed it. I enjoyed being so exhausted, we were all exhausted.

I walked down the slope from the platform with my legs trembling. There was a queue at the till in the Narvesen kiosk, they were people on their way *to* work, not coming home like I was, and they were buying newspapers and *Norsk Ukeblad* and Cokes in the kiosk, and I joined the queue and when it was my turn, I bought *Dagbladet*. I felt strangely important, my body not like the bodies in front of me or behind me in the queue. I was one of those who kept the wheels turning, all day and night, if necessary. In a dignified way I walked towards the exit, up to the glass doors, and outside it was surprisingly cold, still dark, it would soon be winter. I walked on downhill towards the square, Carl Berners Plass, and onwards around the corner to the left, and then the last bit along Trondhjemsveien before it

81

turned to the city centre, and at the junction I went straight to my small flat on Finnmark-gata.

On the pedestrian crossing I met a man I knew. We stopped in the middle of the street; he was older than me, nearly ten years older, and a member of the same Communist Party. His name was Frank. He was a skilled worker in a factory close to Hasle Station, he had roots there going back many years, he had been there all his adult life, and not like me with only two months to show. But of course Frank was not his name, it was an alias, I did not know what he was called. I called myself Arne, it was my alias for Arvid, and I often chose the wrong name because both began with an 'A' and had two syllables. It was hopeless, but I had picked it myself, so I guess I could not change it now. He said:

'Good morning, comrade, you're already off to work?'

'No,' I said, 'I'm on my way home, I've worked the night shift. I live there,' I said, pointing to my window that faced the junction where we were standing.

He turned to look, then turned back.

'So you've done overtime,' he said, and I said yes, I had, I was exhausted, and he said that was good, because night shifts welded the workers together, boosted solidarity and

82

made it easier to be a Communist, he said.

'You're probably right,' I said, but to be honest, I had forgotten to be a Communist that night. I had manned the machine and then messed around at break time and had a laugh with the others. And the one time Hassan was cursing and bashing away with a spanner because a loose, badly folded sheet was jammed at the end of the line and forced the straps and rollers out of position, we played football beside the forklift trucks with a big ball of orange rags we had tied together with elastic bands and string, like children used to do in the yards before the war. The World Cup was that year, and we could still feel the enthusiasm, even though Holland was beaten by West Germany in the final.

A car came down the street and honked loudly, and we were still standing in the middle of the junction, and then Frank whose name was not Frank said:

'Go get yourself some sleep and wake up fit for a fight,' and I said I surely intended to. Then he crossed to his side and I crossed to mine and the car drove past and I walked through the arch and crossed to the stairwell and up the two flights of stairs and stuck my key in the lock.

★   ★   ★

The flat was quiet. It smelled of dust. There was a droning in my head and my body still felt the rasping beat of the machines, thump, thump, thump, my temples were pounding, and my ears ringing. If I went to bed now, I would not fall asleep.

I felt like some coffee, but that would only make it worse. I opened the door to the fridge to see if I had a beer, just a half, but there was no beer, and I did not want juice. So I drank a glass of water. I sat down at the table, rested my head in my hands and closed my eyes and sat like this for a while. Sometimes it troubled me that what we produced in the factory was so completely unnecessary, stupefying even, but I knew that this was not important. It was the work itself that was important.

I stood up and went to the living room to fetch the book that I was reading from the coffee table: Jan Myrdal on Afghanistan, *Crossroad of Cultures*, where lines crossed from east to west, from west to east, caravans of visions and barely audible songs in the thin air. I sat down at the kitchen table to read. There was a wide open sky over Jan Myrdal's sentences. The world unfolded in all its majesty, back in time, forward in time, history was one long river and we were all borne along by that river. People all over the world had the same yearnings, the same dreams and stood hand in hand in one great circle around the globe.

I went into the living room, undressed and glanced at Mao who was hanging there between Bob Dylan and Joni Mitchell before I slipped under the duvet. I read a few pages, and then my eyes grew tired. I put the book aside, I can sleep now, I thought, we will manage, I thought, it will be all right.

9

I got up from the old sofa bed and went to the window. Between our summer house and Hansen's was a well trodden path through the willow hedge and on that path I saw my mother's back and Hansen's back disappear, as my own back and the back of a girl called Inger had done more than twenty years ago on our way to the other side of the hedge to kiss and hug when she had the house to herself. I just presumed it would carry on like this for ever, until one summer I came down and they had sold their summer house and she was gone. I have never really been able to see enormous changes coming until the last minute, never seen how one trend conceals another, as Mao used to say, how the one flowing right below the surface can move in a whole different direction than the one you thought everyone had agreed on, and if you did not pay attention when everything was shifting, you would be left behind alone.

★   ★   ★

I went to the door where my boots were, laced them up and put on my reefer jacket and went outside and around the summer house where the old pine tree stood. Ten years ago there had been three of them, but winter storms had knocked the two over and my father had spent a full summer cutting them into logs which he split into firewood and stacked by the shed under corrugated iron he fastened with a rope against the wind. But the last pine was still standing and refused to be moved or knocked over by any wind and it had grown tall, and more than tall, and its needles and sprigs were thick and dense and blocked the sun in the evenings, and the lower branches stretched out across our roof and creaked and groaned when the wind came in from the sea. My mother wanted it down. She had been saying so for years, she wanted it down *now*, but time went by and my father withdrew from the task, he was no longer a young man, I could see that, and he had my sympathy.

I walked past the gap in the hedge where the path led to Hansen's summer house, and down the gravel road and walked the same route I had walked a couple of hours earlier. It felt ridiculous, as if I was getting nowhere and was only repeating what I had done already.

An elderly woman came cycling past me on her way to town. A brown bag hung from the handlebars and I knew at once who she was. She was the mother of a girl called Bente, that my brother used to know, not my eldest brother, nor the one who came last, but the one who came after me and had already died. It happened six years earlier. That he died. I gave her a nod, but she did not recognise me, or she did not want to, and simply kept going on her black, Danish bicycle, leaving me with the sight of her back. She too had a summer house out here. She lived on the southern side of town, less than one hour away on a bicycle.

Fifteen, twenty metres further on she suddenly put her feet awkwardly to the ground and started braking that way. She nearly fell over, bicycle, bag and all. Then she made a half-turn with one hand on the saddle.

'Is that you, Arvid?' she almost yelled. Mrs Kaspersen was her name. Else Marie Kaspersen in full, but we had never said that.

I walked up to her, stopped by the handlebars of her bicycle and said:

'Yes, it is. It's me.'

'Are you here now?' she said. 'Is your mother here?'

'Yes, she is.'

'I've been thinking so much about her. How is she?'

'She's fine,' I said. 'Just fine.'

'That's good to hear.' She looked down at the pedals. 'It was so sad what happened to your brother. He was such a nice lad.'

My brother, I thought, what brother, I have forgotten my brother, I thought, but of course I had not. I had not forgotten my brother.

'You know, for a long time I hoped he would be my son-in-law.'

'Well, Bente didn't want him, did she?'

'Is that so? I thought he was the one that ended it,' Mrs Kaspersen said.

'I don't think so. Not as far as I remember.'

'You may be right. I don't know. But I wouldn't have minded him for a son-in-law,' she said.

'I know that,' I said.

'It was so sad what happened.'

'Yes, it was sad,' I said, but that was not what I was thinking. I thought, stupid cow, what do you know about sad, what do you know about sad? Nothing, I thought. Nothing.

'I remember it like yesterday,' she said.

'Well, it's been six years now,' I said.

'Has it really been that long?'

'Yes,' I said.

She shook her head and bit her lip, she was

probably thinking about her daughter. Perhaps Bente was not doing that well, perhaps
she had married an idiot. And then I thought:
Maybe she should have chosen my brother
after all, and he would not have died.

'Ah well, the past, no one can change it,'
she said, 'but please give my best to your
mother. Tell her I'll come by if she's staying a
few days.'

You won't come by, I thought. Not you. No
bloody way.

'I will tell her,' I said. 'I promise.' And she
was happy. Then a worried expression fell
over her face like a blind coming down.

'Well, I must not be late. It's a bit chilly,
isn't it. It's November, and all.'

'That much is true,' I said, 'it is November.'
And she said:

'Goodbye then, Arvid,' and I said:

'Take care, Mrs Kaspersen,' and she cycled
off on her black bicycle. I waited until she
had gone around the bend with the dog roses
and then I walked on to the beach.

When I got there, I sat down in the same
spot I had sat earlier that morning, where my
mother had sat too. I looked around me and
saw that the ribbon of reeds had expanded
these last few years and now made swimming
on this beach difficult unless you came
equipped with a large machete, and this

because a small river ran into the sea just north of here turning the water brackish and gave to this stretch of coast a different character. When I was a boy, there was a bridge over the river and the reeds, so we could walk out to the good bathing spots without getting our feet wet, but not even a pole was left of it. Those who wanted to swim had to move closer to town and the beaches there.

I closed my eyes and buried my hands in the sand, and I just wanted to sit here and then I suddenly knew that familiar scent and the air on my skin I had felt down the years in precisely this place, but never like when I was seven years old, even though everything was different then, the season was different, the whole beach was different, no reeds or scrub back then, everything more horizontal, one line behind another, again and again, right out to the last line, where the clouds tumbled like smoke. But this was where we sat, at the foot of the dunes, and it was not yet the Sixties. Straight to the east lay the island with the lighthouse. It was hazy out there, and the lighthouse was not lit up, but I knew every minute where the lighthouse was. I had it in the corner of my eye.

It had been a very hot day, there was a sharp smell of drying seaweed in the air, of half-dead jellyfish baking in the splintering light, the smell of the sea and the prickling scent of marram grass and the tang of newly opened bottles of sweet orange squash. Black-haired and small, I sat with a spade in my hand digging in the dark, moist sand, and all around me were my blond, full-grown, coarse-limbed brothers. There were only two of them at the time, and they were nice, but they took up a lot of space. Every time I turned around, one of them was there.

A man with bare feet came along the path from the north. He had rolled up his trouser legs, showing ankles as white as chalk. He stared as he passed us and then he stopped a few steps further on and looked down at my mother who was lying on her side on a tartan rug in the sun with a smoking cigarette in one hand. She was still not afraid of lung cancer, so the cigarette was a Carlton, not a menthol. In the other hand she held a novel by Günter Grass, a thick one, I recall, that someone must have sent up from Germany: *The Tin Drum*, probably, which had been published that year, it was a sensation. She was tanned in her swimming costume, it was red with blue piping, I remember it well, the crêpe, its sly folds, I often dreamt about it.

'I just had to tell you, madam,' the man said, 'how very charitable of you I think it is to take a little refugee child on holiday within your own family.'

That was how he phrased it and he spoke in Danish, but we had no problem with that, nor was there any doubt which child he was referring to even though I was not so goddamn little that year, and they all turned as one and stared at me, and my brothers looked embarrassed for reasons I did not comprehend. They blushed and my mother smiled, she too a bit awkward, it seemed. But she made no reply, and the man, he raised his hat, a straw hat, I am certain it was, a Panama with a black band, and then he swaggered on, his hands behind his back, barefoot and pleased with himself and the modest lady on the rug and a remark he did not doubt was correct, but where was I supposed to have fled from? From Korea, or the mountains of Tibet? But I did not look Oriental at all, nor was I a refugee from the war in Algiers, and yes, I was dark in those days, but not that dark, so then maybe I was running from Hungary, from the crisis down there? And still there were countries to choose from, but maybe he had no special country in mind, just the fact that I looked different and it was obvious to everyone that I was not like my brothers, and that made me a refugee child, and he was the kind of man who could not keep his mouth shut.

I wish he had never spoken those words on the beach that day. I would never forget them. And no matter how much I came to resemble my father, and no matter how much they assured me that I was not an accident, in fact the only one who was not, *that* in itself confirmed what I had already suspected, that my place in the family was not as evident as I would have wished.

When the man left, my game was ruined. Yet we stayed on the beach for a good while longer and my mother lit another cigarette and returned to her book, but from where I sat in the sand I could see that she never raised her hand to turn the page. She must have read the same lines over and over, distracted, or no longer in the mood, or maybe she was not reading at all, just staring at the printed page. It made me uneasy, things were not as they should be, and the only thing I could do was pretend to play a game I no longer gave a damn about.

But what I found out that summer, the last summer before the Fifties ended and the Sixties kicked off, before the wall was built between East and West, was that I could swallow whatever hit me and let it sink as if nothing had happened. So I mimicked a game that meant nothing to me now, I was going through the motions, and then it looked as if what I was doing had a purpose, but it did not.

ʌ   ʌ   ✶

There was still a path in the sand alongside the reeds to where the bridge had once been, and in some places even right through the reeds, and I stood up, I was thirty-seven years old and brushed the sand off my trousers and followed the path for a while and suddenly I could not see the lighthouse any more or the sea, but only thick, rustling, yellow stems on both sides, like a wall of bamboo, I thought, in China, on the banks of the Yangtze Kiang. So then for a while I was Chinese, my legs trembling like the legs of a weary soldier fighting the Japanese invasion, or like the poet Tu Fu many centuries before, on one of his long and hazardous journeys.

A jetty had been built at a bend in the river right in front of me, and three rowing boats were moored to it, each painted a different colour, red and green and blue. The oars were neatly placed across the thwarts. There was not a soul in sight, on land nor at sea, only the path and the reeds and an open patch of grass in front of the jetty, and I cautiously climbed into the one boat that had no water in it and sat down on the middle thwart with my back against the jetty and the shore. I did not touch the oars, just sat there, very still, looking across the water in the river. It was green and shiny as a mirror in a way the open sea could never be, and I had never felt as unhappy as I did right then.

★ ★ ★

I don't know how long I sat in that boat, but when I stood up from the thwart to step ashore, my body felt cold and stiff. I took a long step over to the jetty, and as I shifted my weight from one foot to the other, I slipped off the plank and right down between the boat and the jetty, and the gap was so narrow that the back of my head hit the side of the boat as I fell. Sparks flew in the great dark inside my brain and it hurt so badly I was scared and when I opened my mouth to call for help, the brackish water poured in and the water seeped into my jacket and my jumper grew heavy and dragged me down. I coughed and spluttered and thrashed my arms about trying to swim, but there was no room. Then I realised where I was, that I could probably touch the bottom, and so I stood up and the water only came to my chest. I could not haul myself up between the boat and the jetty, the gap was too narrow, so I sacrificed what dignity I had left, took a deep breath and ducked under the jetty and with my knees against the sandy bottom moved to the other side and up on to the planks. I lay there, stretched out, until the cold got such a grip of me that my teeth were chattering and I was forced to stand up.

There were two ways out of this mess, one was to go back on the path on which I came, or I could walk along the river, past the houses where the people lived who owned the rowing boats, but I did not want them to see me in the shape I was in, and so I ran back across the open grassy mounds and along the path with the tall reeds on either side, and I did not feel Chinese now, and I ran all the way back and came stomping in my boots past our shed, around the pine tree that blocked the sun and around the corner by the terrace where the door to the living room was open, and my mother stood alone inside with her head bent and both hands in her hair. When she heard me coming she took hold of the door frame, and I could have been the man in the moon or anyone at all by the look she gave me, but then she stared me right in the eye and said:

'But, Arvid, where did you come from?'

Water was dripping from the sleeves of my

97

jacket, from my hair, and I turned and pointed towards the road and the sea behind the trees.

'I came from down there,' I said.

'Oh, dear God,' my mother said, shaking her head. 'That was not what I meant.'

'OK,' I said. I kept looking at her. She didn't look well.

'What are you staring at?' she said.

'You,' I said, 'I'm looking at you.'

'Well, you can stop that,' she said and went into the living room.

10

What Mrs Else Marie Kaspersen had in mind and took the liberty of bringing up was the following.

* * *

My eldest brother called me at work one morning and told me to go to Ullevål Hospital.

'Don't even sit down,' he said, 'just go.'

It concerned the brother who came after me in the queue, whom Mrs Kaspersen so badly had wanted as her son-in-law. That was in 1983. I was working in a bookshop then, in the centre of Oslo, right by the National Gallery. I had been there for two years. Before that I had worked in a factory where we produced a thick slick weekly magazine, and I manned the last stage of the production line for five years. I thought I had to. But I didn't.

I had just got to work when I heard the telephone ring. I switched the lamp on, leaned over the counter and picked up the receiver from the telephone that was squashed between two stacks of catalogues from publishers in England and the US. I was the only one who was in this early. Every day except Sundays and every other Saturday I would come down the stairway at home, run along the footpath between the houses and take my seat on the bus, leaning against the vibrating window all the way into Oslo. I was usually the first one to lock myself into the shop and would happily have gone there on Sundays too. I was happy with my work as I had never been before. It was the first time I would wake up in the morning and think, *I am going to work*, and not feel any reluctance whatsoever. I was so happy in that bookshop that it took me a long time to understand that it was not just the job in itself, but the fact that every morning I could close the door behind me, and just let go.

★ ★ ★

It was not difficult to get to Ullevål Hospital from the street where the bookshop was. I could simply run to Pilestredet, a parallel street, where the trams stopped in those days, and catch one there and it would take fifteen minutes to get to the hospital.

It was early autumn and the sky was clear. I sat by the window in the tram, my face pressed against the glass and looked out at the strange, low sunlight which gave to the buildings a surreal shade of yellow, like in a stage play, I thought, from hidden spotlights, and I could not recall that I had ever seen such an incredibly yellow light, but of course I must have.

I was well aware of what was waiting for me at the other end of this tram ride, but I did not want to think about it yet. I had a whole quarter of an hour I could spend on something else. A whole life could be contained in those fifteen minutes, yes, it was as though that quarter of an hour might never end, but instead expand like a space where nothing *could* ever end, even though I knew that after fifteen minutes, a few seconds and a certain number of stops I would reach Ullevål Hospital and would have to step off the tram to walk the hundred metres on the pavement along Kirkeveien and turn left through the archway in the tower and walk to the hospital block which had my second-youngest brother locked up somewhere on the twelfth floor.

'Take the corridor to the right after the lift, and ask for the duty nurse,' my brother explained on the telephone, 'and say his name loud,' he said in an insistent voice I only rarely heard him use, but I did not know if I could do that, say his name out loud.

But all this would happen soon enough, and I started to think about something quite different in the section of the brain I thought might have some capacity to spare. I believed I could cover quite a few topics if only I was able to concentrate, and the first that for some reason occurred to me was the episode in Hemingway's book *A Moveable Feast* where Hemingway himself and his older more established colleague, Scott Fitzgerald, go to the men's room in a café on the corner of rue Jacob and rue des Saints-Pères in Paris to estimate the size of Fitzgerald's equipment. His wife, Zelda, had spoken scornfully about it and claimed that the happiness in a relationship such as theirs was a question of length, and that Fitzgerald would never be able to make a woman happy the way he had been put together; and now the man was crushed. But in the men's room, Hemingway was able to confirm that everything was fine, you're all right, Scott, he said. But when you see it from above you get a false impression, look at yourself in profile in a mirror, he lectured, then go to the Louvre and look at the statues there, and you'll realise how fortunate you are. And it was not that the advice was bad, but when I read it again after I had turned thirty, the year we are talking about now, 1983, then the first thing that struck me was the condescending tone in which the episode had been written. More than thirty years after Paris, Hemingway still needed to humiliate Fitzgerald, even though Fitzgerald at the time this took place was already on his way down and would end his life practically forgotten, wasted away in alcohol, while Hemingway was on his way up, and would stay there for a long time. It was the sign of a pettiness which recurred in his work, and I especially found the incident in the men's room in rue Jacob painful, as though it concerned me personally, and I began to wonder how much it told about Hemingway's writing, the fact that he could clearly be a bastard, and I think I could have underlined my argument with several examples if the tram I was in had not at that very moment turned past the redbrick buildings that make up the Veterinary College in Oslo. It was on the right hand side of the tramlines on the road through an area of west Oslo called Adamstuen, a part of the city I did not know anything about and I could not have told you where it was, if my life depended on it, had it not been for the one time the year before when I came in a car that was not mine, the long way from where I lived north-east of Oslo, with a map spread out on the passenger seat, going to the Veterinary College to have a dog put down, that also did not belong to me.

I cannot understand why I had volunteered to do this, but I had. It was a bitch that belonged to someone in the family. For reasons that were none of my business they could no longer keep her. I knew the dog quite well and had often taken her for walks in the early morning to help out when things were not easy. I think we liked each other in a distant and polite way, and after all, we had known each other since she was a puppy and I was a younger man. But she also annoyed me, for she was half hunting dog, half beagle, I think, and she found it hard to walk to heel the way I wanted her to. Instead she was the kind of dog who strained and strained at the leash until I felt torn in half from frustration, and if I let her loose, she was gone with the wind. I found that embarrassing, especially if I had to catch the bus into Oslo, and instead was forced to run around calling out for her among the trees that surrounded the suburb where I lived then and still do. And I remember thinking I was glad she was not my dog.

As I turned into the car park of what I supposed was the clinic for animals of medium size, she sat calmly in the back seat gazing out of the window of the car, which was the red Opel Kadett she always rode in.

For once she walked calmly and obediently by my side through the door and over to the hatch where a woman was sitting behind glass looking with her blue eyes so deeply into mine I felt uneasy, and when she asked what it was about, I said it was about putting this dog down.

'I see,' she said, and she leaned forward to look at the dog, and the dog looked back and cautiously wagged its tail.

'You'll have to take a seat over there and wait with the others,' she said, and pointed. It was not necessary, I could easily find my way. I went over and sat down, still holding the dog by its leash, and now I had a numbered ticket in my hand. She settled down on the floor right in front of me with her paws on the toes of my shoes, and I thought I ought to talk softly to her the last few minutes she had left to live, and give her some words of comfort, but I could not think of anything appropriate. Besides, she was calm now, a little introverted even, though there were people on the chairs to my left and right with cats in cages and hamsters and all sorts of other creatures.

After some time a man in a white coat opened a door and called out the number on my ticket. I stood up and went to the door and gave him the leash with the dog at the other end of it, and she followed him willingly. I went back and sat down to wait, even though he had not told me to. What worried me was that no one had asked if the dog was really mine. It felt unsafe, ambiguous, anything could happen, to anyone, if the one it was happening to had a trusting heart.

It took less than ten minutes before the man reappeared in the doorway in his coat, which was still as white as it was before. He called me over. I stood up and walked to the door, and he opened it wide so I could walk past him and he held out his hand in a bidding gesture towards the next door.

'You will want to see her,' he said.

'Yes,' I said. 'Of course.' And as he was still holding his arm out in the same frozen gesture, I walked a few steps and opened the next door. She was lying on a table of brightly polished metal. It looked cold, and she lay keeled over with all four legs stretched out to the same side in a way she would never have done had she been alive and I had never ever seen her so quiet. A dead dog is quieter than a house on a plain, a chair in an empty room.

'There was no problem,' the man in the white coat said.

I said nothing. I wondered if I was supposed to take her back to the car. I could see myself with the dog, heavy in my arms, walking through the room from one end to the other, her fur against my palms, head lolling, ears dangling, on my way past the people waiting on their chairs, but there was nothing to suggest that, so, empty-handed, I turned to leave.

'Thank you,' I said.

'You forgot this,' he said.

I turned back, startled, and then he gave me the leash with the open collar. I took it and went to pay for services rendered, and back in the car I placed the leash with the collar on the seat next to me, on top of the map that was lying there, the area of Adamstuen still circled with a ballpoint pen, and I forgot where it was the moment I left, and I hit the steering wheel with my fist and said to myself, you idiot, why did you agree to see her, why do you always say yes, just because you think you have to, and I punched the steering wheel with my fist, I kept hitting it, and inside the tram I hammered my fist just as hard against the window ledge and we were past the Veterinary College now and I realised that these fifteen minutes I had thought I could inhabit so safely were far from being an expanding space, on the contrary, it was like it always is with time, that it can slip through your fingers when you are not looking.

Shortly afterwards I came to the junction

with Kirkeveien, which is where you get off if you want to go to Ullevål Hospital.

*   *   *

On the twelfth floor I got out of the lift and took a few steps to the right. I did not feel ready. I stopped and stood very still. Something was stuck in my throat and I could not get it out. Right in front of me there were large windows with a view to the north. I went right up to one of them and leaned my forehead against the glass and looked down, and I felt such an unexpected blow to my stomach that I thought perhaps I was going to fall right through the window all the way to the ground. A flush of heat washed through my body, and it was as if a wind came through my head with a deafening blast and all sorts of trash I had long forgotten crashed against the walls of my brain. I spread my legs like sailors do and pressed both palms against the window, and with my forehead still hard against the glass, I held my eyes open and forced myself to remain there, and if a helicopter, maybe with several injured patients on board, had come sweeping past at that moment, the pilot would have seen a man with his eyes and mouth wide open, like a mask pressed against the window a dozen floors up. Then I squeezed my eyes tightly shut and sucked the air into my lungs and held it there for as long as I could, and when I finally opened my eyes, the world stood still.

On the ground, at the foot of the building, a man, or perhaps a boy, came running at full speed past the entrance and around the corner, and shortly afterward reappeared from the other corner and began a new round. There was something vaguely familiar about that figure, but at the same time he looked weird, distorted somehow, seen from the twelfth floor.

Down the corridor I found the office of the duty nurse and said my brother's name out loud through the open door and received a clear answer and a long look in return, and even further down the corridor I found the room where my brother was, opened the door and went right in.

It was not what I had expected. He was the only patient there, and he was on a ventilator. He was lost, I could see that right away, it was not him breathing, it was this machine that pushed air into his lungs in a way no human being had ever breathed, and there were sounds coming from the machine, scary mechanical, hissing noises. The machine looked evil, it was hurting him, it was beating his body, and he could not defend himself, could not stop the hammering, for he was lost. But my mother sat by his side holding his one hand in both of hers, and she was not crying, she only said: 'my boy,' she said, 'my boy,' she said, and she was completely absorbed by what was happening, or had already happened, so overwhelmingly blind to everything else she was, and her boy was this brother of mine who was younger than me, but not the youngest, and who was tall and heavy-set and did not look like me at all, but without a doubt had been important to me in the time that was behind us. And I too must have played some part in his life, in the twenty-seven years we had known each other and had surely exchanged thoughts and done many things together in spite of the years which divided us, but I had forgotten what they were. Big chunks of life had been lost when I entered the room in Ullevål Hospital and saw him lying in the ventilator, fettered and chained like a naked cosmonaut all alone in his cockpit, launched and alone on his way to some small maybe warmer place in the cold universe, if such a place existed, which sadly I did not believe, but I could not recall a single thing we had shared. No confidences exchanged between us, not in recent years certainly, and not when we were children either. And that could not be right. It was all there if only I could concentrate hard enough, but inside my brain there was something inattentive, some slippery patch of Teflon, where things that came swirling in and struck it bounced off again and were gone, a fickleness of the mind. I was not paying attention, things happened and were lost. Important things.

In a chair by the window my father was sitting with something like a smile on his lips, an inappropriate smile, in that case, and he stared out of the window and across the buildings which made up Ullevål Hospital and further on to Ullevål Hageby where the houses looked impeccably English and a tiny bit snobbish, and perhaps he could see all the way to Ullevål Stadium from where he was sitting.

When he turned from the window and looked across the room, he could see me where I stood two paces into the room, and I suddenly realised that he was embarrassed, that the expression I could see on his face, in his eyes, his faint smile, was embarrassment, and this while his third son was lying there dying just a few metres from him, or perhaps was already dead. And I was like my father was, we looked like each other, we were made from the same mould, I had always heard, and just like him, *I* too was embarrassed. I

111

did not know death so close up, death was a stranger, and it made me embarrassed. I did not want to stay. I had just come in, but now I wanted out. I had no idea what to say and neither did my father, and our eyes met across the room, and we looked away at once and it made me feel so resigned and bitter, almost. The wild flush of heat from the window in the corridor had left my body, and my joints grew stiff and my face rigid like a mask, and I looked at the chair where my mother was sitting, leaning over my brother's bed, and I thought if *I* were the one lying in the ventilator here on the twelfth floor in a block of Ullevål Hospital dying, or perhaps already dead, would she then be so unconditionally absorbed by what was happening to me? Would she immerse herself so completely in *my* destiny, or was the shadow I cast not long enough, not substantial enough, for her?

I took two steps back towards the door and caught my father's eye before I pulled my tobacco pouch out of my pocket and pointed to it, opened the door behind me, turned and went out into the corridor. My mother had not once looked in my direction to share with me what was happening.

There were windows on this side too, and a blinding light hit my face. I half turned and searched my pockets for my sunglasses, and I found them and pushed them into place and rolled myself a cigarette with my back against the wall, licked the paper and sealed the cigarette and went to look for a room where I could smoke it, and I found one, further down the corridor, a small lounge behind a glass wall with chairs and a table. But it was impossible to sit down in the state I was in, so I stayed close to the glass with the cigarette between my fingers and drew the smoke into my lungs and forced myself to think about absolutely nothing, which in fact was not that difficult.

When the cigarette was smoked to a stub, and I was about to squash it in the tin ashtray on the table, my little brother rushed past on the other side of the glass wall. He was out of breath, his mouth hung open as he hurried from the lift, and his handsome face looked washed out and swollen and his eyes were puffy. He raced blindly ahead without looking left or right, but he knew where he was going, and I realised that he had already been to the room with the ventilator and had left only to return after running in circles around the hospital block.

11

I met her just a week after I had last seen her
come from behind the shelter on Økern
Station. She came on her bicycle on the
pavement along Trondhjemsveien, or the E6.
I had left a high rise at Årvoll and was
walking down a footpath towards the road,
past the new library. It was dark, I had been
to a meeting on the seventh floor where my
strong and weak points as a Communist were
discussed in a two-bedroom flat next to the
lift. And not only as a political being, but as a
person as well, for you could not separate the
personal from the political. Six party
members were present at the meeting and
two of them were younger than me, they were
still at sixth form college and severe, they had
revolutionary zeal. So did I, but it was not
easy to keep them at bay, and I came out
worse than expected. Now I was walking
downhill from Årvoll to Carl Berners Plass.

Right before the traffic lights she came
from the opposite direction, going *up* the
valley, and I knew her at once. She was
wearing the same blue coat and the same
badge on her collar as I did, it was red and

114

blue with a yellow star in the middle, it said *Victory for the NLF*, in the white circle around it, and her throat was bare, it looked cold, and she knew me too. I could not see her blush, the light was too dim, but I knew she did, and as she cycled past, I said hi, and she braked and stopped a few metres ahead of me. She turned and pulled her coat tightly around her neck, and I said nothing, and then I said:

'I've seen you.'

'Yes,' she said.

I went right up to her, stopped by her bicycle and placed my hand on the saddle.

'I like your coat,' I said, 'I do,' and it was true. I liked it even though it was a bit too short for her. It suggested someone musical, a vocalist in a band, that kind of thing, and then she laughed and said:

'It was my brother's confirmation coat. He only wore it that day, and later he would not even look at it. I think it's great, but it was terrible on him.'

'It *is* great,' I said, and close up she looked very young, she was younger than I had realised.

'You have been confirmed yourself, then, have you?' I said, and smiled so she would not be offended if my question was totally hopeless.

'Oh, yes, I have,' she said, and laughed again, but I thought, she did not say when, and now it was my turn to blush. I blushed often and there was nothing I could do about it, and it must have been easy for her to see. I let go of the saddle. I pointed to the NLF badge and said:

'That's good.'

'I support them,' she said.

'Who?' I said to test her. I guess it was not very nice of me.

'Those who are fighting the American invasion of Vietnam, NLF, the National Liberation Front.'

'That's good,' I said.

'Yes,' she said. 'It is, isn't it.'

'Right,' I said, and did not know what to say next. 'I guess we'll see each other again,' I said, and what I had in mind was the platform on Økern Station.

'I hope so,' she said, and meant something different, and then I told her where I lived. Just like that, address and all. She did not smile, merely nodded, and we went our separate ways.

A week later she came to my door, and kept coming back and now she had been to my flat many times on her way home from school in the centre of Oslo and had drunk tea in my red kitchen, where I told her of things I knew something about, my books, Afghanistan; the crossroads of cultures, about Mao at his desk, about Edvard Munch and the Party, and she told me about her family, and why she hated going home from school. Once she came up from the city and did her homework at my kitchen table, and I sat down to help her and later we talked and smoked till late in the evening, and I think it was the way she held the cigarette between her fingers which touched me the most, how her palm unfolded in front of her chest with a slight bend of the wrist and the glowing tip pointing to the floor, and that night was the first night she did not go home.

★ ★ ★

Some days later the doorbell rang. Not many people came to see me in this period apart from the girl in the blue coat. I had said goodbye to the friends with whom I had shared almost everything for two years, in the canteen, in the smoking room, in the evenings with pints of beer, and suddenly we had nothing in common. I had not made new friends, unless you count the comrades in the Party, and though most of them were people I liked well, I still did not feel close to any of them. So not many people rang my doorbell except Mrs Andersen who always complained about the way I washed the stairs, and this she did because I used Zalo, which was for washing dishes instead of the soft soap, Krystall.

It was just past noon. I got up from the kitchen table where I sat reading a book by the American author, William Faulkner, or was trying to read and, to be honest, William Faulkner was not exactly on my Party's reading list. Nevertheless, I did try, and then I placed a Chinese bookmark between the pages of *Absalom, Absalom*, which was the title of the book, and went to open the door. I looked through the spyhole first as I always did, and there was my mother.

In the two months that had passed, I had not seen or spoken to her, nor had I taken the Underground the few stops eastbound to Veitvet in Groruddalen to see her, not even for a free dinner, like I used to.

In the one hand, on the tips of her fingers, my mother balanced a white paper box, almost like waiters carrying plates between the tables in fine restaurants, and she simply looked straight at the door with this smile that was not a smile on her lips. I was certain she was not looking at the spyhole, so hopefully she was not aware that I was inside watching her. The white flat box was level with her ear; and it was autumn now, she wore her grey coat and the red scarf around her neck. She would soon celebrate her fiftieth birthday and was younger then than I am now, sitting here, writing this and that feels strange to me. I thought she looked great.

But something important had changed. There was a *before* and an *after* in time, a border which I had crossed, or perhaps a river, like the Rio Grande, and so I suddenly found myself in Mexico where things were different and a little frightening, and the crossing had left its mark on my face, which my mother would instantly see and realise that now we were standing on opposite sides of that river, and the fact that I had left her would hurt her, and that's why she didn't like me any more, did not want me. *Get thee behind me,* she would say, *you idiot.*

★ ★ ★

I could always pretend I was not at home, that I had gone to a matinee at the cinema or gone shopping or might still be at work, in that case on the morning shift, but this she would have checked in advance, and anyway, I had longed for her. So I opened the door.

'Hi,' I said.

'Hi,' she said, 'so there you are,' for I had kept her waiting a long time.

'Come in,' I said, and stepped aside. She crossed the threshold. She was neither calm nor irritable, but had that slightly impatient, let-us-put-an-end-to-this-nonsense expression she often wore. We went through the small hall and into the kitchen. It was the only room I kept tidy, the other room contained all the things I owned and they were piled high, I have to admit.

'Are you broke?' she said.

'No,' I said. 'Not really.'

'No, I don't suppose you are,' she said, and placed the white box carefully on the kitchen table. She threw a glance at *Absalom, Absalom*, which was still lying there.

'It's hard going, that book,' she said.

'I agree,' I said, 'but it's a fine book all the same.'

'Of course it is, but I never got through it, I'm ashamed to say,' she said, and to tell the truth, I would never get through it either, I was sure of that. Still it felt good to read, even though I would never finish it. This was the strange thing. It did not matter.

With three fingers she opened one end of the white box and pulled out a small cardboard tray with two Napoleon cakes on it. I stared at them. I did not know what to say. I did not know if I should feel glad, or embarrassed.

'From Bergersen's,' I said, and she replied: 'No. They're not.' And then she said: 'Don't you have any coffee?'

'Of course.'

'Then put the kettle on, and let's get started.'

I did as she told me, and it was as if I were incapable of doing anything, unless she told me what to do. So I put the kettle on, and I saw that she was looking at my hands to see if they had already changed, and of course they had, they were raw and peeling and a bit black under the nails, and she noticed that, and my body was still aching from all the abrupt movements and the heavy lifting I was not used to for so many hours, every day around the clock, that's how it felt, but it was not something I was going to talk about unless she asked me, and she did not.

I looked at the clock above the door and saw that the evening shift did not start for another three hours. So there was plenty of time to sit here and eat cake and then go to work, to Økern, two stops to the east on the Underground, which was the same place my father worked for many years right from when I was little, where he no longer worked, for he could not cope with the noisy shifts, with the buzzing and the dust every hour of the day, week after week a new shift in the body, he felt jetlagged, he dropped cups on the floor, plates on the floor, his stomach couldn't take it and the thirty kilometres of skiing he had done every single Sunday his entire adult life was suddenly too much, and not one single Sunday could he do it.

'Shouldn't you be at work now?' I said.

'Where? At Freia?'

'Yes. Where else?'

'I don't work at Freia any more.'

'I didn't know that.'

'No, how could you,' she said.

I put three tablespoons of coffee into a filter, poured the water, and I stood there waiting until the coffee was ready, looking out the window towards Finnmarkgata and the nearly bare trees on the hill called Ola Narr, and I looked at the windowsills I had painted a clear and luminous shade of red and I knew I would have to paint them white again if I were ever to move, and I guess I would, one day. I poured the fresh coffee into a flask which was as orange as the windowsills were red and placed it on the table and was about to sit down when she said:

'Cups and plates,' and I had barely sat down before I had to get up again and fetch the cups and plates from the cupboard. I opened the top drawer in the kitchen counter and found a spatula I used as a cake slicer whenever I had some cake in the house and placed it next to the two Napoleon cakes and sat down, and that seemed to be fine with her. She took the spatula, carefully lifted the two cakes on to the plates, and then she stood up after all, went over to the counter, opened the top drawer and came back with two forks.

'Right,' she said, 'let's taste these cakes and then we'll say no more about it.'

Say no more about it. And we hadn't said a word. She cut back to a point before anything had happened, and there was nothing wrong with the cakes, I had not tasted any better in a long time, and we are talking about an expert here, *me*, that is, and we were well into autumn now, outside the window came the wind in great spirals of dust and leaves from chestnut trees, maples, and lime trees, and the tarmac looked harder than it did in the summer, like a crust you could fall on and really hurt yourself. But in my kitchen the heat rose from a radiator, up my legs and to my stomach, and the radiator too I had painted red. But really it was too late. It suddenly struck me. That it might be too late. She should have come earlier, or I should have taken the Underground to the house with the thin cardboard walls you could kick a hole in so your foot would crash into your neighbour's living room, and I realised that she too knew it, that it might be too late, and she knew that I knew, but as long as we didn't talk about it and ate our Napoleon cakes, we could keep that knowledge at bay. Nor had she come to apologise, she had come because I was her son. That's how it was. She had come because she was a *mother*. And yet it was too late. Something was broken, a wire had been stretched too taut and had started to fray and it snapped with a crack you could hear between the walls. And I knew she heard it as well as I did.

But the ball was in my court, and there it could not stay. So as a joke, and to inject a little humour into the shiny red kitchen, I said:

'So did he kick you out, the foreman at Freia?' and I smiled because I did not think such a thing could really happen.

'No,' she said. '*I* kicked him.'

'*You* kicked him?'

'Yes, on the shin. Quite hard, actually, and then I left. For good.'

'But you can't just walk out on a job like that? There are rules, aren't there? You must have been there ten years, you'll lose all your rights.'

'Frankly, I don't give a shit about that, if

you pardon a mother such an expression,' and I guess I could excuse an expression like that, but I knew that my father would never have done such a thing, nor would I, even though *I* was the one who had thrown it all away and left a college where I learned the things I had always wanted to learn, and was now an industrial worker, like she was, and my father was, but they, of course, because they had to.

'So what are you doing now? I mean, have you got yourself another job?'

'I'm a maid at Park Hotel,' she said harshly, and looked me in the eye with a defiant stare, as though I was someone who might be condescending about that kind of job, but I did not even know what a maid was, and said so, and then she said:

'I hoover rooms, make beds, clean toilets and so on,' she said, and I who had not spent a single night in a hotel in my entire life, understood that what she did at the Park Hotel was the same as she had done in the flat on Veitvet and always had done and always hated, and that is what I said, I said:

'But Mother, you've always hated that kind of work,' and she said:

'That's true, but now I don't really mind. Now I'm paid for it, and that makes all the difference, doesn't it?' And, of course, there was a difference.

And so there we sat, she and I, on either side of the table in the kitchen with the red painted windowsills, eating Napoleon cakes, with a view of Finnmarkgata and Ola Narr and nothing more, right between the Munch Museum and Carl Berners Plass, and the room fell silent, we said nothing, nor did we look at each other, and I started to think about all the films we had seen together, on TV in black and white, or at Sinsen Kino, at Grorud Kino, at Ringen Kino, right up the street from where my flat was, and an evening ten years ago came to mind, when we had gone to the Colosseum Kino in Majorstua in Oslo, just she and I, to see the film *Grand Prix* with Yves Montand and James Garner starring as the two racing drivers. We had dressed up for the occasion, she in a blue dress with yellow flowers, I in my grey Beatles jacket, without a collar, but trimmed with narrow black ribbon all the way around, and early into the film I was already a big fan of Yves Montand. He was firm and determined behind his wheel, but he had something more, something in his eyes, a sadness maybe, which James Garner did not have. *Do you ever get tired? Of the driving,* Yves Montand said. *No,* said James Garner. *I sometimes get tired,* Yves Montand said, but perhaps this sadness was nothing more than the fact that he was French, and my mother could easily understand why Yves Montand was my favourite.

But he died in the film. He died the very moment he realised he was about to find the happiness he had so longed for, with Eva Marie Saint, who might have taken that sad, French look from his eyes, and then he swerved off the track in a sea of burning petrol, and I covered my eyes, I sobbed my heart out, and when we left the cinema, my mother had to stop by the car park on the way to Majorstua Station to comfort me. And then we heard the *vrooom* from the cars in the car park where grown men elated by the film revved their engines before popping the clutch so the tyres spun on the tarmac and gave off a screeching sound and then turned out into the wide world. A bit too fast, a bit too hard in the curves, chasing the pure line, and then, of course, they just drove home. My mother laughed, loud and bubbly, almost lovingly, I thought, in her dark voice, and *I* laughed too, loud and enchanted, in my high-pitched voice, I was still only a boy then, my eyes filled with tears, and I looked up into her face for I understood what was going on, I understood why the men revved their engines like that after seeing the film, and *she* laughed because she thought they were childish, but also because she loved them for doing it, and if we had had a car, she and I, we would have done the same thing, skidded around the corner of the car park with a roar, and driven through the streets of Oslo, she and I, with me at the wheel.

* * *

'Do you recall *Grand Prix*?' I said.

'The Eurovision Song Contest?'

'No. I mean the film we saw together, you and I, at the Colosseum, the one with Yves Montand.'

'And James Garner? Oh yes, I remember it well. It was exciting. Fast cars, Monte Carlo, the whole works,' she said with a faint smile. 'But he died in the film, Yves Montand. It was so sad, you cried like a whipped dog. But it wasn't just you and I, was it? Surely your brother was there too?'

And suddenly I remembered. That my big brother was there, that we sat either side of her in the wide, tall dark that was the Colosseum Kino. It was *not* just she and I, because my brother had been there too, and so all three of us must have been stood in the car park when I cried like a whipped dog, which I am certain my brother did not, when the elated drivers, so inspired by the film that they revved their engines before popping the clutch, had vanished down the street in a roar and rounded the corner on two wheels, at Majorstua Station. But my brother was not in the picture I carried with me from that evening. I had erased him at once. Like Stalin erased Trotsky.

★   ★   ★

And then it was over. We had eaten the Napoleon cakes, scraped the plates clean, and both hands on the table she stood up and folded the small cardboard tray four times, crumpled up the white box and threw them in the bin.

'So, will we be seeing you on Sunday? For dinner. Your brothers are coming.'

'Yes,' I said, 'that sounds great. Unless I have to go to a meeting.'

'I see,' she said, and she stood there with her back straight as a board, and maybe there was something she wanted to add, but if so, she changed her mind, and I followed her through the hall and opened the door, and without turning once she went down the stairwell where I had washed every single step with the Zalo, instead of Krystall soft soap.

III

12

Some weeks before I sailed to Denmark on the old, rundown ferry, the *Holger Danske* to seek out my mother, I found a letter in my letterbox among the junk mail and the two newspapers I had subscribed to since I left home more than seventeen years earlier. I opened the letter and sat down on the second step of the stairwell outside my flat, just left of the letterboxes. My behind grew quickly cold, but it is the place I always sit down when there is something urgent I have to respond to and I thought this might be one of those occasions.

Inside the A5 envelope was a postcard with an art motif on the front. On the back of the card a woman had filled all the available space in a handwriting that must have been formed some time in the Fifties.

This is how the text began:

On Saturday October 28th we passed each other at Oslo Central Station. A brief moment. I wore a black cap with multicoloured pompoms. Then I saw how much you look like your father, as I remember him. I grew up in Vålerenggata 5 — right across the

133

landing from your family. *I remember them well. Your father, your mother — her especially.*

She had signed her name, a name I had never heard of or seen, and below it in brackets she had written 'nee *Frantzen*'.

Vålerenggata 5! The square apartment building on the corner of Smålensgata and Vålerenggata, where the tram went past. I remember the old dairy there, with tiles on the floor, and walking past you could see through the archway to the clothes lines in the backyard where white vests were hanging like dead men, like corpses, while my father's checked shirts swayed, always waving at me from the washing line. To the left after the entrance you reached the first stairwell with a door and a small window of safety glass and then up the stairs to the second floor with that special smell lingering between the walls, which I thought had something to do with my grandfather, his clothes, his brown jacket, the polka dot bow tie he always wore even when he had taken his jacket off, or his shirts, his brown shoes, something he had in his hair, something viscous in tiny bottles with snuff-coloured labels, but there were seven families living on that stairwell, including the caretaker on the ground floor, so surely he alone could not be responsible for that smell.

For all I knew every single stairwell in Oslo smelled like that. They said he was a good man. A good Christian. Personally I could curb my enthusiasm. As could my mother.

It said *Frantzen* on the door across from us. I recall the metal letterbox that opened out and not in and the spyhole way above my head. The Frantzens' door was the first thing I saw when my mother and I came hand in hand up the stairs after a trip to the shops or a ride on the tram up from town, and our bodies felt a mutual resistance, like some electric current passing from one arm to the other and back again down our legs, that made them hard to lift, and the reason I have always remembered the nameplate was the 'z' — a letter I thought was used only by Zorro.

The Frantzens' door was to the right on the second floor and ours was to the left. My grandfather's name was on our nameplate. His middle name Adolf had been reduced to an 'A', which was no surprise, in the years after the war. I am named after him, I have his first and last name and I have always hated them. But the *Adolf* in the middle I escaped because the vicar in our church put his foot down.

Behind the door with the *A* in the middle lived my mother and my father, and two of his brothers and their father, who was my grandfather, and then my older brother and me. There were two rooms and a kitchen, and they were not very big rooms and the kitchen was not a big kitchen. The walls of the flat were dark in a way that today I would describe as murky, and the blinds were nearly always down. I do not know why. Someone must have thought that shutting the light out would keep the rooms cooler.

I had no idea that my mother knew the people across the landing where it said Frantzen with a 'z' on the nameplate. I never saw anyone coming out of that door or anyone going in, but of course I did not notice everything, I was quite small when we moved from there. Helter-skelter, I later thought, under cover of darkness, in a lorry heading for Økern and Bjerke, and up through Groruddalen, towards the woods and the light, towards Vesletjern and Alunsjøen and Breisjøen.

Sometimes when my father and the other men in the flat had gone to work at the Salomon shoe factory on Kiellands Plass, then someone might ring the bell of our second floor flat in the middle of the day and my mother left the room where my brother and I were sleeping top to tail on the couch, and she looked through the spyhole, to see if the man on the other side was not too grim or too creepy, and if he wasn't she opened the door and let him into the hallway where he was allowed to sit on a chair beneath the coat pegs. She went into the kitchen and made him a lunch bag. The men who rang the bell were always unshaven, men with no work or money, in scruffy coats from before the war, men without homes who slept under trees and the bushes at night, in the park by Vålerenga Church, in the doorways of Galgeberg and Enebakkveien by the US style petrol station on the corner of Strømsveien, or the big house on the bend where the Salvation Army War Academy was based, where Christian men in uniform practised sabre attacks on the third floor, in their socks, I liked to imagine, to protect the parquet flooring, and more than once my mother gave the men who rang the bell an old pair of shoes, if they were in want of one, and they often were.

When I was little I used to imagine that one of those men might be my real father for I often felt that this would solve a problem I had, if somewhere out there was an unknown and unnamed father still wandering the streets at night in his old coat and the shoes my mother had given to him, restlessly, impatiently searching for a place where *he* would fit in, just a small place, where *I* might be, where *I* might be sitting in a dark corner with my thighs against my stomach and my forehead resting on my knees, barely moving, barely breathing, waiting until one night I would hear his steps between the houses and know them at once. And even though I stopped fantasising like this several decades ago, it hit me hard reading the first few lines of the postcard I received from the woman born *Frantzen*, with a 'z', from Vålerenggata 5. I knew I looked like my father, but no one said so any more. No one had mentioned it for years. Probably because they were all dead now, the people who knew we looked like each other.

I did not *want* to look like him. I did not *want* to look in the mirror and see my father there. But from early on I realised that the day would come when everyone could see how much I resembled my father. It would separate me from my mother for good. Even though the two of them were married. And shared a life. But that was not how I saw it. That they shared a life. And it would tie me to my father for good because I looked like him and perhaps thought like he did, and against my will would find myself on the other side of the great divide, the great chasm where he lived in the murky twilight among the crammed furniture, where his father was with his Adolf in the middle, and his brothers, who were my uncles, a small crowd of gloomy men standing shoulder to shoulder nailed to a place where my mother did *not* belong, because she was different from them, because she had been carried away to this place, and so in some strange way was free.

Wherever she went my brother went too, the eldest, for he was the unwanted child, a child born in secrecy and shame off the coast of Denmark, among the marram grass and the grazing sheep on an island called Læsø. She had travelled there in haste with my brother like a shimmering fish in her belly, and it bound them to each other with an ease which did not embrace me. He had sunshine and pain in his body inside the foamy blue and glittering room where he was so safe and so unwanted, like an outlaw, and the first thing he saw in his life was a sheepdog roaming the heath and gulls soaring above the port and the vault of blue sky above the island. The first thing *I* saw was my father's face and three grey, scrawny pigeons on the dusty windowsill behind the dangling blinds and the tram on Vålerenggata. I was the only one of four sons who was planned, who was wanted by them both, and they told me this, time after time, and each time as good news, as something to celebrate, and it gave me a

139

legitimacy I could have done without. I longed to be an outlaw like my mother was, and my brother, to be with them and share their pain and in secret wander the dark streets at night in search of a place where *I* could belong, I would open the door to strangers and hide behind a mask like Zorro did, because it did *not* come easily to me, what the two of them shared. It scared me. So, as the years passed I became the Lone Ranger, looking for unsafe ground, and I clung to her, did tricks for her, performed for her, pulled laughter out of her with my silly jokes whose punchlines were lost in linguistic confusion. As soon as I opened my mouth the sentences came tumbling out at a shocking speed, I stayed in nappies longer than other children to tie myself to her, I could spell before I was out of nappies. But no matter how hard I tried, I was still like my father.

★ ★ ★

Nothing in the world was obvious to me back then, in Vålerenggata 5, nothing was simple. So I kept a sharp eye on everything around me and I should have noticed that the woman whose body had once been so strong, so robust, at some point grew thinner and thinner, that her lap was no longer so soft.

140

But I did not warn them, did not shout: *'Danger!'* to the men in the flat who were all equally blind, for I was a late talker and knew only a few words of Norwegian at that age, so she had to work it out for herself, the pain, the weight loss, her random periods, and she had to drag herself off to a doctor, almost furtively, with my brother and me in tow, and leave us in waiting rooms where there was nothing to play with, not even Lego was invented yet. And there we sat, my brother and I, dangling our legs, staring at one another, or I sat on his lap and he showed me the pictures in *Norsk Ukeblad* or sometimes *Illustrert* and waited for what seemed like a lifetime, while *she* lay in there, cringing with shame, her legs in stirrups behind the soundproofed double doors, and the doctor finally pushed back his chair, took his glasses off and said:

'I'm sorry, madam, let me be straight with you. This looks like cancer. We'll see what we can do. You have children, don't you?'

'Yes,' she said. 'I have children.'

* * *

When the three of us came home from our secret mission, to Sagene, I think, or maybe Bjølsen, the men were still at work, and as she had cleaned and tidied the flat before we left some hours earlier, my mother went across the landing to see Mrs Frantzen who was home from work and now sitting in her kitchen with her daughter, who almost thirty years later would send me a letter.

My mother sat down by Mrs Frantzen's table and she buried her face in her hands and started to cry because she was exhausted, because it had been such a long ride back through town from Sagene or Bjølsen with my brother and me in tow. And Mrs Frantzen, who knew about my mother's condition, said:

'So, my lass, how did it go?'

And my mother said:

'I've got cancer, I'm going to die.'

'You don't know that,' Mrs Frantzen said. 'Many survive. And you have children.'

'Yes,' my mother said. 'That's true. I have children. I have two children. And in their brief lives they've barely had room to move in the flat across the landing, and now they're going to be without a mother to take care of them and give them what they need and I've neglected them so badly.'

'No, you haven't,' Mrs Frantzen said. 'You can't say that.'

'Yes,' my mother said, 'I can say that, and they've never even tasted chocolate. Not once,' she said, and that might have been true, that we had never tasted chocolate, but in that case it was not something we held against her. But from that day onwards she stuffed us with chocolate. Freia milk chocolate and Kvikklunsj bars, and every day was like a celebration, and then she would cry a little because she was going to die soon and would not be able to spend with us the years to come, the years that were queuing up one after another, but all the same it was a party, and she carefully put away the chocolate wrappers in small paper bags and threw them in the neighbours' bins, just as she carefully washed our faces before our men returned from work.

And then she did not die. She lived on and had two more sons, and I do not know how it was resolved, if the diagnosis was wrong or a successful operation was performed that I was not told about, or whether she was simply worn out by the twilight life with all those men behind the blinds on the second floor, and the weight started to drop off her and that the life she was leading was making her ill. You cannot rule that out, because shortly after we quickly moved from this place, from the flat on the corner of Smålensgata and Vålerenggata, where those damned tramlines ran, and up to the new and more affordable housing at Veitvet, which was completed that year, or at least our terraced house was, and my father came with us, but he only, and within a short time she felt much better and almost looked like her old self.

13

I felt so cold. I was drenched. I followed my mother from the terrace into the living room and tugged at the reefer jacket, got the buttons out of buttonholes that were too small and pulled the jacket off and hell, it was hard work. She turned her back to me and I threw all my clothes on the floor as the water ran down my thighs. I rummaged through my bag and found no spare clothes, no trousers, no jumpers or shirts, but what I did find was writing equipment and notebooks with Chinese signs on the cover and secrets written down inside them, right back from the mid-Seventies, and no one ever knew about those notebooks, not even the girl in the blue coat, not one member of the Party, and I had kept them in my pockets all this time, in many different jackets, in leather jackets, army jackets, reefer jackets. *I can't take it any more*, it said in one of them on an otherwise blank page, *so stupid*, it said. *It is too late*, it said on another page, but I could not recall exactly what it was that was too late. At the very bottom of the bag I found a blanket I had really no use for, as you were no longer allowed to sleep on the benches on the deck of the *Holger Danske* the way I used to. These days you had to pay for a cabin if you wanted to take the night ferry to Denmark, and besides it was too cold to lie under the open sky far out at sea in November, so when I packed the blanket it was more out of habit.

I took out the blanket, and with all my clothes in a soaking pile on the floor, I wrapped it tightly around me, and it was hard to breathe, I would catch pneumonia, no doubt about it, my head was pounding, I felt wretched. I kicked my clothes and was so confused and temple-throbbingly furious, but she had done me no harm.

Tilting her head, she studied me closely where I stood in the middle of the floor, water dripping from my hair, tightly wrapped in my blanket, and she should have given me a towel then, but she did not, and maybe just then, there was a smile on her lips, an ironic smile or any smile at all, but perhaps that was only wishful thinking. She went to the bedroom and opened a wardrobe in the corner and came back with several garments over her arm which I knew belonged to my father. I had not seen them in years, not since I was young and my body was younger and my father was younger and his body really filled those clothes. There was a charcoal

146

jumper with red trim, a T-shirt that no longer had any colour and a pair of trousers that once upon a time had been beige or khaki, like a British uniform in hot and sun-scorched colonies, but they had faded now after decades of hardboiled washing. But the colour was not the point. The point was that when I had put on those clothes with shy and awkward movements because this time my mother did *not* turn her back to me, they fitted like a glove, as if they were made especially for me. But they were not. They were meant for my father and purchased especially for him twenty years ago or more. And it was good to feel dry, warm clothes against my skin, but it was also odd to wear clothes that fitted so well, so comfortably, and yet belonged to another man.

'That's what I thought,' my mother said. 'That they would fit.'

★ ★ ★

I had not eaten that day, not on the ferry, no breakfast of crusty Danish rolls and Danish butter and delicious full-cream milk and coffee, I had not eaten a Kvikklunsj, or milk chocolate from Freia, and the dry clothes made me feel drowsy and dizzy, floating aimlessly about as if I were drunk.

147

'Why don't we eat,' I said, 'you do have food here?'

'Of course I have food,' she said.

'Well, let's eat then,' I said.

She looked at me, turned and opened the fridge, and I went to the cupboard above the kitchen counter and took out plates and cups, as I had done when I was small and a good little boy in her presence, and I smoothed the tablecloth to both sides with the palms of my hands and tugged it slightly at each end and set out cutlery on the table. She fried eggs on the stove, and I heard her hum, or quietly sing, a soft Elvis song: 'Are you lonesome tonight' it was. Then she fried the bacon and toasted bread in the chrome toaster we had had on the kitchen counter since the dawn of time and switched on a fan above the stove which was so noisy it was impossible to talk. And that suited me fine.

We sat at the table to eat. It felt good to sit down. I closed my eyes and opened them. It was an effort. It was like breaking cardboard. I lifted my cup and drank a mouthful of coffee. I had not tasted anything that good in a long time.

She looked at my hands. 'What's wrong with your hand?' she said. I put the cup on the saucer and looked at my right hand. My knuckles were red and slightly swollen. I opened my hand and closed it again, clenched it hard. It hurt. I told her what was wrong with it.

'Oh, for God's sake, Arvid,' she said. 'When did you start getting caught up in that kind of thing?'

'I haven't. He was coming at me. He made up his mind the moment he saw me in the bar.'

'I hardly think so,' my mother said.

'I guess that's for me to know,' I said. 'I was the one who was there.'

'There's no doubt about that,' she said.

When our plates were empty, I said:

'Maybe you would like a drink now? A Calvados?' I attempted a sly smile, as if I were joking, I mean, it was only one o'clock in the afternoon or something and I was a little startled when she replied:

'Yes, please, I'd like that,' she said. 'Why don't we have it on the terrace?'

'Now? Won't it be too cold?'

'We'll wrap our duvets around us.'

OK. We will wrap our duvets around us. I stood up. And then I got all excited and took the bottle from the table by the window and took two medium sized glasses from the cupboard behind me and went outside to the terrace in the cold and placed them on the picnic table and poured two decent sized shots before I went back inside. She was waiting with the duvets. I took one, shook it out a bit, and then we went outside and sat in our chairs to drink Calvados with our duvets wrapped tightly around us. She was wearing woollen gloves. It was so cold our breath streamed from our mouths like frosty mist.

The glasses were on the table. She lit a cigarette, there was a smell of singed wool, and she said nothing, and the glasses stayed where they were, and I did not drink when she did not. I eased the blue packet out of my pocket and rolled a cigarette with stiff fingers. I smoked making no noise and just stared into the distance. After a while I leaned forward to look out across the big meadow stretching from the back of our plot towards a farm on the other side. There used to be horses in that meadow, and heifers sometimes. I had flown kites in that meadow when I was a boy, but it was a wilderness now, and the grass was so tall and dense there was no way you could walk through it unless you were a roe deer on its long legs. And there were hares and hedgehogs, too, and pheasants with chicks that were full grown now, in November, and rodents in abundance, and hawks in the sky above, and buzzards that came sweeping out of nowhere, and falcons hanging cruciform in the air before hurtling down, and there were owls in the oak trees in the evening, all quiet where they perched on a branch in the dark and stared their prey to death, and in the black night a marten darted between the trees and up across our roof, and there was plenty to eat for everyone.

I threw the cigarette stub on to the lawn, and then I raised my glass anyway, said *skol* and took a sip even though her glass remained untouched on the table, but then she too raised her glass and said:

'Well, *skol* then, Arvid,' and took a large gulp and coughed violently and said: 'Bloody hell, that was strong,' and then she said: 'Oh, that's good booze! Imagine, to live so long and still have that in store!'

⋆　⋆　⋆

Then we just sat there. For a long time she was silent and her breathing was wheezy, and if you listened carefully, you could hear her taking great pains to keep it going, and eventually it was her breathing that made me drowsy. We lay in the deckchairs with our eyes closed and the duvets tightly around us, so only our heads were free and our right hands free to hold the glass. And I could picture us looking like TB patients at Glitre Sanatorium in Hakadal, on the terrace with a view of the valley, or in the Alps in Switzerland. But it was not TB that ailed my mother. Nor me, if you could say that something ailed me. It felt that way.

'Are you feeling better now?' I said.

She did not reply.

'Yes,' she said.

'So am I,' I said.

Then out of the blue she said: 'Do you remember little brother?'

I thought, little brother, of course I remember little brother, why did she say it like that? I grew scared, had something happened to little brother that I did not know about? Surely he was OK where he was, he was in Norway, he was in the last year of his apprenticeship with a plumber and he was different from the rest of us brothers. He did not want to go to college, he hated school, he did not read books, he was dyslexic, and I liked him very much. He was little brother, he was the last one, not him who came after me, who had died.

And then I realised what she meant. Across the meadow a dog came hopping on stiff legs in the tall grass and landed just about half a metre further on each time, it was an Alsatian chasing something that was moving deep below the roof of crested wheat grass and thistles. I had seen a fox leap that way once and thought it was a rare sight, but clearly it was not.

'The dog, you mean?'

'Yes,' she said.

★   ★   ★

Every year when we came down on the ferry, an Alsatian called Teddy would be waiting for little brother on the other side of the hedge. The dog knew precisely when we came, when *he* came, it had a sixth sense, that maybe only dogs have, and it would grow restless from early in the morning and would pine to be let out of the house and press its nose against the hedge until we arrived from the ferry to the summer house in our own car or in a taxi.

As soon as we opened the car door, Teddy would storm through the hedge and throw himself at little brother, sending him sprawling, and little brother would knock Teddy down and get back on his feet and hurry inside to change. A moment later he reappeared in shorts and trainers and together they raced down to the beach and all the way up to Strandby in the north and back again, and damnit, that was a long way. Two hours later they would run up along the hedge, both exhausted and throw themselves on the grass, panting and gasping. They would do this almost every single day. He loved that dog.

'Out of all of you, he's the best looking,' my mother said, and maybe that was true, but I felt it was wrong of her to classify us in that way. Then she said: 'Teddy couldn't live for ever. It's sad, really.'

'Yes,' I said, 'it's sad,' and it was true that little brother was the best looking. Once a lady had stopped him on Karl Johansgate and asked if her sister could take a photo of them together. Several people stopped and stared, and when he told us about it at home, he blushed, but right now all I remember was his body against mine, the substance of it, the trust, and the few words he said over and over again were the only words he knew, and my name was one of them, and I would not let him go.

'He'll never learn to walk properly,' my mother said. 'Put him down, for God's sake.' But I did not put him down, and he did not want me to.

14

The empty glasses were on the table, she rose with an effort and rolled up the duvet in her lap and was already on the way to her room. She squeezed her eyes tightly shut, opened them, and I rose and blocked her path and said:

'Are you feeling unwell?'

'Yes,' she said.

'Is there anything I can do for you?' I said, but she raised her hand and said:

'If anything needs doing, I'll do it myself. Get out of my way,' she said and pushed me in the chest.

'But, Mother,' I said, 'why won't you let me do something for you? I want to.'

'Well, that seems reasonable,' she said, 'but it's not going to happen. And we'll say no more about it.'

And we will say no more about it, and my eyes were stinging and my legs were burning, and she pushed me aside and went into the living room and on into the bedroom and closed the door and it fell silent.

I followed her and stopped outside the door, just staring at it. I turned and looked in the mirror that hung on the wall by the bathroom, and I did not like what I saw, did not like those eyes. I felt restless. I took the two glasses from the table outside and put them on the kitchen counter, moved them to the sink and I filled the sink with hot water and a dash of Zalo and I washed the glasses, and the cups and the plates from breakfast, and everything else I could find I washed and stacked in the cupboards and I carefully wiped the kitchen counter, wiped the tablecloth, and then there was nothing more to do.

She had gone to bed in such haste that she had forgotten the book she was reading, *The Razor's Edge*, and that was unusual for her, but she did not call out to me to bring it.

I went over to the big window and pulled the curtain aside and looked across the meadow. I could not see a single animal, not a single bird of interest. Beneath the clouds the sun came in low across the tall, pale, withered grass pushing long shadows out from behind the tiniest objects, and far across the meadow, where the farm was, white smoke came swirling from the chimney of the main building. The barn was chalk white in the blinding light. A man came on his moped along the road to the farm. He had a helmet on, although he was not going very fast, and the light caught his mirror, and the puffing sound from the small engine cut sharply through the autumn air and could clearly be heard, even behind the window where I was standing holding the curtain. I bent down to add a couple of logs to the rumbling fire and put my boots on even though they were still damp, and I ticd the long laces around my ankles and went out on the terrace, and there I stood in the cold, slanted November sun, shining on the grass in front of the summer house.

I looked across the meadow. Smoke was still coming from the chimney, but the moped was gone. I turned and walked along the hedge and then on the path leading to Hansen's plot. I bent double and slipped through the hole in the hedge and walked around his summer house, which was barely bigger than a shed, and there I found him hunched over an outboard motor he had attached to the sawhorse. He heard me coming, straightened up and turned with a monkey wrench in his hand and smiled his strange, fine and toothless smile.

'Jesus Christ, you look just like your father,' he said, and his voice made the air quiver.

'I know it,' I said.

'Especially in those clothes,' he said. 'For a moment I thought . . . you know what I mean.'

I did, but any answer I could have given him had been used up long ago. He sat on the edge of his terrace, put the monkey wrench down with that dry little sound only a monkey wrench makes, and wiped his hands on a bright orange rag, which he then stuffed into his back pocket.

'I'll never get this piece of crap running again,' he said.

'Why, what's wrong with it?'

'I really don't know,' he said. 'I've tried everything. It just won't start. So I guess I'll have to row instead.'

Hansen was no athlete. He looked like Andy Capp, but in a lovable way. He used to put eel traps in the river and sometimes he fished for plaice from a small boat with this outboard motor attached to the stern. He had had it for years. He never bought anything new. He preferred simple tools, antique outboard motors, a small moped. Old things, used things, things with uncomplicated mechanics, things he had bought from people he knew from the railway. Buying something new seemed senseless to him. He never had any money, and I don't think he even found money interesting.

'Well don't row too much, then, it may ruin your health,' I said, and that was not much of a thing to say, but it was all I had, and then it fell quiet and Hansen said:

158

'Listen, Arvid my friend, tell me something. Is it true that you're getting a divorce?'

'Yes,' I said. 'That's correct.'

'Jesus Christ. My condolences.'

'I don't know,' I said. 'I don't think it kills you.'

'Don't be too sure,' Hansen said. 'Anything can happen. Let's have a beer,' he said. He stood up with a groan and went inside his shed through a ramshackle glasshouse, the orange rag hanging from his back pocket like an angry flag, a railway flag, I thought, for explosive cargo, trains of thought, maybe: Lenin on the train on his way home from his exile in Geneva, heading for the Finland Station in Petrograd, and Hansen shouting: Look out! Look out! But he was not that old, of course. Instead he swiftly returned with a bottle of beer in each hand. He passed me one, it was cold in my hand, and I said:

'Long live the people,' and then I said: 'Down the hatch!' And we drank deeply, and then Hansen said:

'That didn't hurt none.'

The wind cut through my clothes as I sat on the edge of the terrace, my hands were cold. The trees around us were bare now, hazel and oak and beech trees were bare, and willow and alder, and ancient plum trees, and all kinds of other trees, and they were all stripped of their leaves. And the wind came from the north, from the town of Skagen, from icy Norway with its spruce forests and granite, and my father heading along winding paths for he did not know where else to take his body.

Hansen waved me over and said:

'Come, let's enter Crystal Palace. We can take off our coats in there, if that's what we want to do.' And it was. He had an electric heater which was red hot behind the mesh, and it sent waves of heat out into the room, and we sat down on white plastic chairs holding our shiny green bottles of beer. I raised the bottle to my mouth and took a big swig, and with the Calvados already in my stomach like a small bullet, it tasted so good. I might start drinking, I thought, drink often, every day, just to feel like this, close my eyes and feel the alcohol flowing through my body. I closed my eyes. Crystal Palace was quiet. It was warm. Only a low fizz from the bottles and some gulls above the trees outside could be heard.

'Your mother,' Hansen said.

'Yes,' I said, but I kept my eyes closed.

'She's ill,' Hansen said.

'I know,' I said. 'That's why I'm here,' and it went quiet, and he said nothing and then I said:

'That's why I've come. Why else would I at this time of the year? It's not summer exactly,' I said. 'I wasn't planning to get a tan or anything.'

'No, it's not summer, that's true,' he said.

I opened my eyes. On the wall there was a large framed picture of the *Christian Radich*, fully rigged on the ocean blue, in the Bay of Biscay perhaps, or in the North Sea on her way to Newcastle. My mother had given the picture to Hansen many years ago, for his fiftieth birthday. Next to the picture was a bookcase, packed with novels by John Steinbeck; a handsome two-volume edition of *East of Eden*, and *Three Comrades* by Erich Maria Remarque was there too. I had read it before I turned twenty, and one called *Heaven Has No Favourites* which I had read too. It was about a racing driver and the woman he loved, who had TB, and was now staying at a sanatorium where he often went to see her, in the Swiss Alps, *Bella Vista*, it was called. There was always a woman with TB in Remarque's books. Frankly I was a little fed up with it.

★ ★ ★

I stood up with my beer in my hand and went over to the small bookcase and took out

161

Three Comrades and looked at the fine jacket with a colourful drawing of *Karl, das Chaussegespenst*, which was the name of the racing car they owned, the three comrades, who were the characters in the book. And then there was the woman with TB, the fourth comrade, as in *The Three Musketeers*, which was not about three characters either, but about four, and the fourth was D'Artagnan.

'How is she doing in there?' Hansen said.

'She was tired,' I said, 'she has gone to lie down.'

'I can understand that. Would you be offended if I did the same?'

'Did what?' I said.

'Lie down for a bit?'

'Are you ill as well?'

'No, I don't think so. But I'm tired, I am, and not as young as you.'

'No, of course not,' I said. 'You go and lie down.' I took two steps towards the door thinking, does he want me to leave?

'That's what I'll do then,' Hansen said, and then he got up and drained the rest of his beer, and said: 'You can stay here where it's warm. You're always welcome.' And he went into the bedroom at the back of Crystal Palace with his revolutionary cloth still hanging from his back pocket.

Always welcome. I stood with the bottle in my hand. I did not know if I should go or sit down again and maybe read a bit of *Three Comrades*. But the air was heavy in there, too warm, and there was something wrong with the book. I felt cheated.

I quickly left Crystal Palace, taking the beer with me; I might as well go home to Norway, I thought. Nobody wants me here.

I crossed the small terrace and walked past the sawhorse with the outboard motor on top, and as I turned to look back, there was a pheasant standing dead still in the stripy shadow of a leafless bush, its strange, long tail feathers pointing towards the road, and it was brown and green and red within a silence so compact I found it menacing. Only one shiny eye was moving inside its red frame and it followed every step I took, and this eye frightened me.

'Jesus Christ,' I said. 'It's an omen,' and on my way through the hedge I could feel the eye burning into my back.

15

It was Saturday, it was just before midnight. I was walking along Trondhjemsveien towards town after celebrating my mother's fiftieth birthday. I had made up my mind to walk all the way home to Carl Berners Plass even though I could easily have got there in less than fifteen minutes by Underground, but I had to get the party out of my system.

It was a long way to Carl Berners Plass, the night was dark, but the street lights lit up the road, and some were yellow and some almost orange, and some had a cold, blue glare.

I had walked this road for many years, but before I left home, I nearly always walked in the opposite direction, *out* of Oslo, because I wanted the traffic to flow *with* me on the side of the road I preferred to walk, the right hand side that is, and if I did not, it would feel like the people in the cars, looking out of their windows, and rolling their windows down, would point at me, and say to each other that I was probably the only person in the whole world that was heading in the wrong direction with his life.

But I no longer lived in my parents' home,

I had not lived there for three years. Now I was walking into town one late autumn night after my mother's fiftieth birthday party, towards central Oslo, past Årvoll and further on under the Sinsen roundabout, down past Torshovdalen and the Rosenhoff School standing grey and sad at the end of a street to the right. I had been a pupil there two years before I went on to college. The building looked like a seventeenth-century prison, like the Bastille in Paris, and my time at that school had not been a time of joy. But now I put the school behind me along with those years, and walked on down the long slope towards Carl Berners Plass.

When I finally got there, I thought, as I often did, what a fine square it was, like a sun beaming out to all sides, like a square in the years between the wars, in a big city, Berlin perhaps, Erich Kästner's Berlin in *Emil and the Detectives*, or in Zurich, or in Basel, or in Budapest, for all I knew, where trams and buses criss-crossed in carefully designed patterns of shiny steel curves in the cobblestones, and above me in the air, raised high above the traffic, above the tram cogs and rubber wheels, a myriad taut cables ran from the buildings on one side of the street via beautiful metal posts across to the opposite side and were attached to the

165

buildings there. It was like a roof you could walk under without getting your feet wet. It felt like that.

The whole square was a world of its own with the broad majestic avenue, Christian Michelsens Gate, to the west; the green lime trees in straight rows either side of it, or, like now, with their branches bare and grey against the grey night. To the east, Grenseveien sloped up the hill past the Underground station where it vanished beyond the houses, and there were neon signs on the façades of the buildings on Grenseveien, and neon signs around the corner, towards Finnmarkgata, and across the square towards the petrol station there were neon signs too, and to the right or the left, depending on which way you came, lay Ringen Kino with its glowing stripes of red neon above the entrance from Trondhjemsveien, on the same side as the bookshop, but after the film you would come out, half-blind, into Tromsøgata right opposite Bergersen's café.

I felt better once I was on my way across the square, my head no longer spinning, it was late, it was night, the dark whirling around me, and snowflakes whirling in the wind from the north and the traffic was sparse on the streets into town. So here I could walk in the middle of the big square as long as I wanted, across the cobblestones and tramlines, it was my square, it was my big city square, known as Red Square before the war, as the only one of its kind on the east side of the river, and later in the Seventies was called Red Square, because almost everyone was convinced the traffic lights here were always that colour.

★ ★ ★

In the stairwell the fresh scent of Zalo met me on the ground floor, and on the first I turned the key in the lock and entered my flat. Carefully I eased the door shut behind me, so that nothing could be heard but the low click of the latch.

I knew right away that she was there, sensed it in my gut that she was there, my stomach lurching and trembling and to stop that sensation from going away, to hold on to it for as long as I could, I went straight to the kitchen in my socks and did not say *hello* through the half open door to the living room, where the sofa bed stood behind the bookcases.

I had given her a set of keys. She could come and go as she pleased. Do her homework here when she wanted to. Come here early on the Underground before school if she wanted to and have breakfast with me. She could take a break from her family and cry if she wanted to, take a break from the train journeys to school, to the city centre because she always had to step out of the carriage at Økern Station and run behind the shelter there to throw up, and then throw up at Hasle Station. When she had stayed the night with me, and I walked her to the tram at Carl Berners Plass and then again walked her all the way up to school, she would throw up behind the colonnade at the Deichman Library. Once I had been waiting at the entrance to the station right by the block of flats where she lived, and had seen through the window her mother punch her in the face because she put on the wrong coat, which was her brother's blue confirmation coat, on her way out to join me. We were going to see *Klute* starring Jane Fonda and Donald Sutherland. It was showing a second time at Frogner Kino. I had seen it before, but she had not.

Silently, I placed my keys on the kitchen counter and silently I took a bottle of orange juice from the fridge, poured myself a glass and sat down at the table where the book I was reading, *Les Misérables* by Victor Hugo, was lying. I had finished the first volume and was well into the second.

I drank the juice and leafed through the book to remind myself of what I had read in bed earlier that morning, it was a Saturday, I had been lying under my duvet reading until around half-past eleven with the book on my pillow. This was not what I usually did in the morning, but I felt it was important to work through as many pages as possible before the day got going and the time came when I had to take the Underground six stops up through Groruddalen to celebrate my mother's fiftieth birthday.

I undressed in the kitchen, hung my clothes over one of the chairs and went to the small bathroom and washed the whole evening and the party off my skin, brushed my teeth and tiptoed into the living room to the sofa bed behind the bookcases in the dark and around the table stocked with more books. On the wall was the picture of Mao at his desk, but I could not see him now. Carefully I crawled under the duvet. This sofa bed was really not made for two, but we did not need that much room, and I had planned that she would carry on sleeping in my arms and then wake up in the early morning wondering when it was I'd come back. But she was so warm under the duvet and I was so cold that she woke up at once, turned to me and said:

'Is that you?'

'Of course, it's me.'

'OK, if you say so.'

'Stop it, you're making me jealous.'

'Am I?'

'Of course you are,' I said.

'That's good.'

'But, it's just you and me,' I said, 'it's just you and me against the world.'

'Oh, yes that's true,' she said, 'that's it. You and me, you and me, and then your Party. Which I'm going to join.'

'Yes, you are. But you're still a bit young.'

'Perhaps. I don't feel young.'

'I know,' I said, 'and in a way you're not young,' but she *was* young. Several years younger than me, and I was young too, and I leaned across her and rubbed my hands together to make them warm and said: 'Feel this,' and then I touched her in a very special way, and she lay completely still, and then she said in a soft voice:

'Oh God, that was good,' and this very thing, this very special thing, was something only she and I had together, that no one else had, that only she and I knew about, but we were so young then, and we did not know very much.

'But hey, there's no time for this now,' she said. '*Oh God, that was good.* How far have you got?'

170

'Quite far. A lot further than the last time you were here.'

'Oh, that's good,' she said, and we lay on our backs, shoulder to shoulder, hand in hand looking up at the ceiling, and we could not see the ceiling because the room was pitch black, and the sofa bed so small that she was squashed against the wall, and my left leg dangled over the edge. And then I started to tell the story from where we had stopped the last time we were lying here and had to stop because I hadn't read any further, and she told me to hurry and read some more because it was so much better to hear me tell the story than reading it herself, she could see things then, that she did not see when it was light, and I had read on as quickly as I could. And now we were lying here again, like so many times before, and I told her about Jean Valjean who was sent to the gallows for stealing a loaf of bread. But one day when there was a fire he escaped, and was free and changed his name and identity, and as a different man he rose through the ranks to become mayor. And then suddenly he had to run a second time because that hateful, persistent bloodhound of a police inspector Javert had recognised him.

In the novel it was 1832, and that night I told her how Jean Valjean was stumbling through the catacombs under Paris, the sewers of Paris, with Marius unconscious on his back. And he was the boyfriend of his beloved Cosette, and in the streets above, the revolution was raging, the *peuple* were fighting in the streets, the impatient ones, it was their turn now, and *they* were as we were, or rather we wanted to be like them. And the *peuple* built barricades between the houses in the narrow streets, for this was before the time of avenues, avenues that later would be built and made so wide it would be impossible to build barricades from one side to the other, which is the whole point of a barricade, and instead made room for the army to march forward in wide columns and crush the slightest attempt at rebellion, which is the whole point of avenues.

She did not sleep like children do, at night when you tell them stories. She was wide awake in the dark with her blue eyes, warm hands and a greedy mouth, and she said:

'It must have been so hard to carry Marius all that way through the sewers even though Jean Valjean was strong.'

'Yes, I'm sure it must have been. There is no way I could ever do the same,' I said.

'Don't tell yourself that. You're quite strong, you are.'

'Do you think so?'

'I don't think it,' she said. 'I *know* it,' and I liked it when she said things like that.

When I had finished today's text, or the evening's or even the night's text if you like, I was quite exhausted and she said:

'Can we eat now?'

'I have to get some sleep, if you don't mind. I'm totally worn out after that party.'

'Why don't you tell me about the party? How did it go? Did your mother like your present?'

'No,' I said.

I had not bought her a present. I had written a speech, but when it was time for me to stand up, I was drunk.

'Oh, well,' she said. 'That's all right with me, but I need to eat something. It's strange, but lying here listening makes me so hungry.'

'You get yourself something to eat,' I said.

'You get yourself some sleep,' she said and patted my cheek, and she climbed over me on the sofa and before she had touched the floor in the dark, very blonde, very slender and very young, I was long gone.

16

That morning I had been lying in bed reading Victor Hugo until I could no longer stay in bed without feeling ashamed, and so I got up, had a shower, and walked barefoot and wet out into the kitchen where I stood in front of the table reading the speech I had left there. I had read it through several times. I had written that speech instead of buying her a present, it was an idea I had, that I would reach out my hand, and not just an idea, I really meant it. I would say something about the Rio Grande, how big it was, how it kept continents apart, cultures, and was so wide that it was hard to cross from one bank to the other, from the USA to Mexico, that is if you weren't a gunslinger desperately running from the law, so it was easy then to imagine the problems we had had in the past, she and I, standing on opposite banks, not even able to call out to each other across the great divide.

'It's called the Rio Grande, right?' I was going to say. 'That means big, huge, enormous,' and then I would say, but the good news, Mother, is that the river has dried up. It's a total surprise, all the experts are knocked out, and only a trickle remains so now it is easy to cross, for there has been no rain this autumn, not this summer, nor this spring,' I would say, and laugh, 'so you see, nothing's too late for us, we can walk right across or meet halfway and only get our feet a little wet, and that's not a big deal, is it?' That was what I intended to say, and that was what I had written on the two A4 sheets.

I pulled all the clothes I had out of the closet and lined them up on the floor. They were surprisingly few, but I could not turn up for a fiftieth birthday party in the shabby army jacket I normally wore. I chose the dark tweed jacket my mother had given me as a present once when I had to look decent, at the funeral of one of my father's many brothers. He was the uncle who stayed on in the flat in Vålcrenga after our escape to Groruddalen. A bachelor smell lingered between the walls there, of the same meals week in week out, year after year, of the same brand of coffee and the same shoe polish and washing up liquid, of the same vests and underpants in the middle drawer of the cabinet, of chocolate bought for one person only, crumbly and white with age on the top shelf, and in the bottom drawer there were brown socks neatly folded, every single pair of them bought from the Salvation Army. He had lived there until he died on the sofa, in the darkly lit living room among all that furniture with the cream-coloured blinds lowered so that only needle-thin stripes of light seeped through. But two years had passed since that funeral, and I had not worn the jacket since.

I hung the coat hanger with the tweed jacket on the toilet door, folded the two A4 sheets to A5 size and put them in the inside pocket and went down one floor in my socks to the letterboxes and fetched a book in a brown cardboard parcel; *For Whom the Bell Tolls*, I think it was, by Ernest Hemingway, the first of two volumes, then, and at the same time picked up the two newspapers and the green invoice for my rent, which was still 170 kroner.

* * ★ * *

It was Saturday. I took the Underground the few stops from Carl Berners Plass, Hasle, Økern, Risløkka and beyond, the tall red Siemens building and the Østre Aker Vei to the right down the valley and the railway line to the right and the shunting yard to the right by Alnabru, where goods wagons rolled one after the other very quietly along shiny tracks in parallel rows or just stood strangely still, wrapped up in themselves, waiting their turn.

The sun was still hanging over the ridge to the west, but in the valley it was dusk already, was the worst time of year, nothing but dark and rain, and the low clouds above the shunting yards sent a woolly reflection towards the ground below, but between the railway tracks you could not find your way.

In all the years I lived in Veitvet, I had heard through the open window the goods trains moving out there in the night, heard the sound of steel wheels on tracks of steel and the long mournful song from the brakes, and then heard the wagons click into place behind each other, hand in hand, I used to imagine, shoulder to shoulder, a sound of comfort.

I got up from my seat before Veitvet Station and headed for the door. There stood a man I had been acquainted with for many years. He was the father of a boy in my brother's class, the one who came after me, not the one who came last.

The man greeted me, and I greeted him.

'Hello,' he said, and I said:

'Hello.'

'You've moved,' he said, and I said that I had, 'but you're getting off here anyway,' he said, 'at this station,' and I said that I was,

177

and the train stopped and the doors opened. And then I did not get off. He got off, but I stayed there, with my hand clenching the pole till the doors slammed shut. He stopped outside, turned and gave me a puzzled look through the window and suddenly he raised his fist and hammered on the door, shouting something I could not make out, but his face looked tight and contorted. For some reason the man flew into a rage, it's true, he was furious.

I pushed my mouth close to the glass and said with exaggerated lip movements:

'Go to hell. You fucking idiot,' and the next step would probably be sign language, so I raised my hands and made some gestures I thought might look like sign language.

The man was still standing there with his hands on the door, but the train was leaving the station, so he had to let go, and I sat down, my temples throbbing and my breath stuck in my throat the four stops to Grorud Station. There I got off and walked up the steps from the platform and stopped at the top with the Narvesen kiosk behind me to the east and a view of the tracks to the west. I rolled a cigarette and smoked it right down to my fingertips before I walked down to the platform on the opposite side to wait for the westbound train which was due only five minutes later, and when it arrived I got on. This time I did not sit down, but instead clutched the pole tightly and stood with my legs apart as if the carriage was a ship, heaving high and falling hard and pitching against the waves like ships do in the North Sea when the weather is foul, and this time I got off at Veitvet Station.

I walked down the stairs and out of the station behind the shopping centre and the bowling alley, where the same old dopeheads drifted aimlessly in the doorway where they always came together and smoked cigarettes with God knows what kind of shit in them and talked senseless, meaningless nonsense, and some of them were still wearing the same tattered Afghan coats they had always worn, wrapped tightly around their chests in the raw air.

★   ★   ★

Suddenly I felt how ridiculous it would be to give a speech with only the five members of my family present, it would feel too transparent, too intimate. My mother and father did not have many friends. I could not recall a single time when I was little or in my teens that someone came to visit who was not family, only aunts, uncles, those kinds of people, or my grandfather from Vålerenga who was a Baptist preacher at the weekends and a worker in a shoe factory the rest of the week, and after that a pensioner until he keeled over the same year and the same week as King Haakon VII died; or that my mother and father had ever said they were going for an evening out and would be home late because they were meeting friends in town. At a café or in the cinema, or in their friends' homes; at Lambertseter or Bøler, Oppsal, places like that where they might have known someone, given who they were and where my father worked. But they did not, they were not friends with anyone from those places or any other place that I was aware of. My father's brothers with their wives did call on rare occasions and every other Christmas my mother's childless sister came up from Copenhagen acting upper class with her husband who worked in a firm importing French cars and was the creepy owner of a 8mm camera he used for all kinds of things, and my grandparents would also come, their palms worn and hard, from another, more puritanical town in the same country, in the same fashion, by ferry, grey hair, grey clothes, standing windswept and grey on the quay waiting for my father to come down along Trondhjemsveien in a rare taxi to pick them up and sometimes I, too, was in that taxi and they looked so small next to their big suitcases.

★   ★   ★

I passed the nice-looking, red telephone booth and came to the slope where as children we risked our lives on toboggans running down the steep road between the houses, blue woollen caps pulled down over our ears in a childhood whirled away by time, and then past the bend down to Rådyrveien and further on along the terraces, down the flagstone footpath and at last through the door to my parents' flat. The wallpaper in the hall was the same as it always had been, the same mirror, the same hat shelf which no one ever used except for storing boxes with long-forgotten mittens and forgotten scarves. I slammed the door behind me, but the sound was drowned by a wave of noise that came rolling towards me in the hall. In the small kitchen to the left I saw relatives from two countries, from countryside and town in both of them, standing between the table and the cooker, and some even sitting on the kitchen counter, either side of the sink, and in the living room there were neighbours from our own row of houses and the houses next to it and sitting on the stairs to the first floor, like doves in a dovecot, were people I had never even seen. They held glasses in their hands and cigarettes between their fingers, and there was laughter and talk in every corner. The old flat had expanded to all sides as far as it could.

* * *

My aunt from Copenhagen handed me a welcome drink. She still looked upper class in a languorous way and sexy in her tight black dress, even though she was past forty and a little too fond of her drink. I had never liked her. She made the rest of us look like idiots.

There was champagne in the glass and I had no idea where they found the money for champagne, but I knocked it back and took another glass from the tray on the sideboard, and when we sat down a little later to eat, each at our name card, I had drunk a third glass.

A neighbour stood up to bid us all welcome, he always called me *Arvars* for some reason, but it was well meant and really quite pleasant, in fact, we were fond of each other, so I didn't mind being Arvars to him if he found it amusing. He was a lorry driver with a passion for trotting horses, he had owned one himself before he moved up here, and on behalf of my mother and my father, who really should have been the first to speak, he welcomed everyone to this fiftieth birthday party to celebrate a woman who was so close to their hearts, who was one of them, and yet was not quite like them, and maybe that was what they liked about her. That she spoke of other things than what they were used to, about other phenomena, as he expressed it, and she probably did because she was Danish and read a lot of books, and thank God for that, said our friendly neighbour, for they could get rather monotonous, the conversations that took place out on the doorsteps after dinner, about the same dull subjects over and over again, he said. It could not be denied. So then it was good to have my mother sitting out there, with her Carlton cigarette, her secretive smile and her surprisingly deep laughter. Besides, she was not above giving good advice on the complexities of the illicit still the neighbour in question kept by his kitchen sink or sometimes down in the laundry room, in the old tub in the basement where it bubbled and gurgled away up to three times a year, and he did not know where that knowledge came from, if it was something you could learn from reading thick books in a foreign language. The whole L-shaped table erupted in laughter, and I laughed too, quite loudly in fact, and my mother did not blush at all, but sat very still on her chair with a smile on her lips and her hands in her lap next to her husband, my father, who was smiling shyly at the wall on the opposite side of the room.

All this and more said the neighbour, who called me Arvars and whom I liked very much. I had never heard him talk like this before, nor since, for that matter: he was witty, elated even, and laughter wafted up and down the table, and when he rounded the whole thing off with a joke that had nothing to do with anything, which we had heard a thousand times before, the one about the two Lapps, it was a very crude joke in fact — what did they have in their laps? — he took his glass and raised it to the ceiling and proposed a toast for my mother, and then everyone raised their glasses high and drank, and I think I was the fastest drinker of them all.

There were no more speeches, not that anyone expected one. It often grew awkward and silent around them, so when I stood up in the narrow gap between the table and the wall behind me and tapped my knife against my glass, which was empty already, everyone turned in surprise and smiled cautiously in my direction. They must have dreaded what was coming. Every single one of them knew that I was no longer a student at the college on the corner of Dælenenggata and Gøteborggata close to Carl Berners Plass, where my mother had more or less forced me to attend, and this because it was something she would have liked to do herself had it been possible. It had been a hot topic in two countries, and in this house, from doorstep to doorstep, the fact that I was now a Communist, a Maoist, even, which was something they had heard about only on TV, that I wanted to be part of the working class, which, for Christ's sake I already was, and always had been. The whole point, for them, was that I should *stop* being working class so they could all be proud of me, because I had been allowed to go further. They wished me well, they liked me, and I liked them.

Just as I was about to speak I realised I was drunk. I had not eaten that day, had no appetite or had simply forgotten to, and now I had downed three glasses of champagne on an empty stomach, and a glass of wine. So when I stood up, a roaring wind blew through my head, there was spring tide and breaking surf in my brain, I took one step to the side and bumped into a chair where a farmer in a suit was sitting, he smelled of cowshed and milk, an uncle, no doubt about it, I had seen him before, and I had nothing against that smell, on the contrary, it reminded me of childhood, not *my* childhood, but somebody's childhood, and not only was I drunk, I had forgotten the two sheets of paper with the speech in my jacket, and my jacket hung in the hall with the other jackets. It was so hot inside the house now that no one had their jackets on, and to go out into the hall and fetch the speech was out of the question. It was too tight a squeeze. It was too embarrassing. Too many people would have to stand up, and besides, I had already tapped my knife against the glass.

I was going to say something about the Rio Grande, that I could remember, but I could not remember *what* about the Rio Grande, what it was about that river that was important, and then I let it go and felt the consonants fill my mouth so awkwardly that I would not be able to pull them out in whole pieces. My mother looked at me in an almost dreamy way, slightly out of focus, I thought, and she waited, and my father stared at the opposite wall, and he was not the only one.

I steadied myself on the chair of the man next to me. I did not feel well. I had not said anything yet, but I needed a pause. I looked for my glass to take a sip, but I could not find it, and besides, it was probably empty. Next to me, Uncle Farmer saw my fumbling hand, so he took the nearest bottle and poured a fair amount of wine into my glass and slipped it into my hand. I looked down at him, and he nodded and smiled faintly, and I nodded back, he was one fine uncle, the best I had, no question about it. I took a big swig and put the glass back on the table. I opened my mouth, stood like that for a good while before I closed it again. No sound could be heard, not a glass moved, not a knife, not a fork. I tried to concentrate, but I was drunk and it showed, and I looked down at my plate and rubbed my eyelids with the back of my hand like I used to when I was little, and that was it for today, goodnight goodnight.

'Was there something you wanted to say, Arvid?' my mother said in a mild and enquiring voice. I knew exactly how she looked.

'I don't think so,' I said. 'I don't remember anything about you,' I said, 'nothing at all,' and then she said:

'That's probably just as well.'

I looked up and saw my eldest brother at the far end of the table. He was staring at me, he was furious. Perhaps it was time to leave, but I did not know if I could. I took a sip from the glass. I leaned against my farmer and sat down, and then I held out my hand and he took it in his and shook it like farmers do.

'Sorry,' I whispered, 'I don't think that went very well.'

'No, it didn't,' he said. 'But next time I'm sure it will be better.'

I turned to look at him. Suddenly I couldn't recall the last time I saw him, or if I ever had seen him.

'You're my uncle, aren't you?' I said.

'No,' he said, 'but that's all right.'

★ ★ ★

I did not leave right away, but I do not remember the rest of the party very clearly, I do not remember if I said anything to anyone, or if anyone said anything to me, and it is possible that no one did, all things considered. When I finally realised it was time to leave, the clock in the kitchen showed well after eleven. That I do remember.

In the hall I found my jacket with the folded speech in the inside pocket, I opened the door and stepped outside. I went down the flagstone path in the cold, bracing air, and decided then and there to walk all the way down to Carl Berners Plass.

17

The chill from the sea across my face. Clouds drifting. I felt cold inside my father's sweater. I stood with my back to the hedge and Hansen's summer house, and I was thinking about Inger, whom I had kissed behind that hedge. I remember her mouth, how it tasted strange, almost good, but I did not know what to do next. I was thirteen years old and she was fourteen, and we lay in the loft reading Nick Carter books. Nick was smoking in the living room. He looked out of the window. He turned and stubbed out his cigarette in an ashtray with a button in the middle you could press down and it would spin and the butt would disappear. Nick crossed the floor and pulled the blonde up from the sofa, carried her into the bedroom and threw her on the bed. 'Wouldn't you like to be in his place?' Inger said. 'Yes,' I said, but I had no idea what she meant.

★ ★ ★

I might as well leave. But there was no ferry until the next day, and my mother was

189

sleeping, and I did not feel like sitting in a chair waiting for her to wake up. I looked at the pine tree. Its twisted top. The branches scraping against the roof in the wind. I finished the beer and put the bottle down in the thicket at the foot of the hedge. Suddenly I knew what to do, and I decided to start right away, and when I had finished, she would wake up, pull back the curtain, look out while resting her forehead against the glass and suddenly feel elated as she had not done for a long time and at first she would not grasp that this had something to do with *me*. She would look out of the window and instantly see what it was that had changed while she slept, and then she would realise that I had been able to do what my father could not.

I opened the creaking door to the woodshed, and light fell on the tall chopping block in the middle of the dirt floor with an axe planted in it, a new cleaving axe my father had been given for his fifty-seventh birthday. He was still strong for an old man, but I was stronger than him, and had been for a long time, and he knew it.

There was another axe in the corner. Its shaft was shorter and its head was rusty. We had used it for splitting wood before, but now there were deep dents to its edge, and the shaft was fraying where it joined the head. No one had sharpened it, no one had looked after it for a long time. But this was the one I wanted to use. I put on some workman's gloves and took the axe and a spade and a hoe along with me as I left, and a hemp rope that was hanging on a hook I also took and went over to the pine tree. I had not done this before, I had not taken down a tree with roots and all, but I had once seen Hansen do it, before winter, to a tree he thought looked menacing. I got hold of the bottom branch which stretched out across our roof and climbed up and took the end of the rope with me and tied it around the trunk a fair bit above its middle and secured it with a knot I had learned as a Boy Scout twenty-five years earlier. I did not remember much from my Scouting days, but the knot was still in my fingers.

I sat up there on a branch. I ran the rope through the crook of my arm and down to the ground where it fell in a coil. I took off my gloves and tugged them under my jumper and rolled a cigarette and lit it with the blue lighter. I inhaled the smoke deep into my lungs and sat in the pine tree, on the branch, with my back against the trunk, smoking. I squashed the stub against the trunk and let it fall. Then I sat there for a while longer.

I looked down on to Hansen's plot. It was deserted. He was not there. The pheasant too was gone. The outboard motor was white and still attached to the sawhorse. I looked across the roofs of the summer house towards the sea. There were stripes of foam from the north wind, and it was crinkled like a piece of dark cloth or crêpe paper, and it looked numbingly cold, and was lilac in a forbidding way, the horizon a bright white and the sun shining out there, but here it was gone. The sky was low and grey. The wind was getting up, a cold wind hit my back, and around me on all sides the wind came through the pine tree. I don't know what happened. Maybe I passed out briefly, but when I came to, my face was soaking wet, my hands tightly around the rope and my knuckles white. I wiped my face, rubbed my eyes hard with the palm of my hand, put on my gloves and climbed down carefully, one hand on the branches, the other around the rope. I abseiled like a mountaineer, and at the foot of the pine I passed out again, hit my forehead against the trunk and came to at once.

I took a deep breath and then another one and checked if I could use my right hand. I opened and clenched it, and it did hurt a little, but no more than I could cope with. I took the spade and started digging a circle around the trunk in the sandy soil. I felt dizzy, but this was what I wanted to do. I dug another circle, inside the first, and another circle to get deeper down, and then a fourth, a slightly wider circle, and the fifth time the spade hit the root. I dug on and made an even wider circle, and more roots appeared, shiny red and white against the spade.

I sat down to rest with my feet in the trench I had dug. I pulled the gloves off and rolled another cigarette and lit it with my lighter and smoked it all the way down with my eyes closed. The cigarette tasted strangely good. It made me smile.

I lifted my legs out from the trench and stood up and reached for the axe. It felt good in my hands. I swung it a couple of times, like I had seen people on TV swing golf clubs, and then I drove it hard and aslant into the first root, and it snapped just from the speed of the axe head, and I hoped that the sound would not wake my mother. But I guessed she was too exhausted, too tired and unwell, and the axe rushed deep into the sandy soil and must have dented its edge even more but I didn't care. I worked my way around the trunk, and some roots yielded right away while others needed many blows, and most were tough and filled with sap down from the core of the earth and would not let go. But they *had* to let go. There was no mercy and I swung the axe from left to right until nothing hung together any more.

I straightened my aching back, picked up the rope and walked the fifteen paces to the woodshed and dug both heels into the ground. I leaned back with the rope taut from high up on the trunk, and pulled as hard as I could. I heard it creak and felt in my arms how the pine tree started to give and bend towards me, but then it swung back and stood like it did before. Each time I pulled, the same thing happened, and I thought: maybe this will not work, I thought, maybe not, and when she wakes up and pulls back the curtains and looks out, then nothing will have changed, nothing will have happened, and everything will be as it always was.

I let go of the rope and went back to the pine tree, raised the spade and dug even deeper under the tree and slowly the biggest root became visible. It had dug itself straight into the earth like an anchor. I dropped the spade, then clutched the handle of the axe, and I whacked it full force, and hit with a bang, and the axe recoiled. A pain shot through my forearms which went numb at once, and I let the axe fall and I shouted out: 'Goddamnit, I can't take any more', but I did not know what it was I could not take.

194

When the pain died down, I fell on to my knees and closed my eyes until everything inside me fell into place, and I rubbed my hand against my chest and shook my head and got up to have another go at a different angle, and it took me more than twenty blows, but then the root cracked with a subterranean metallic singing sound, as though a wire had snapped down there. I walked towards the shed where I picked up the rope, braced myself, and then I pulled with all my force, and it toppled at once, and the whole pine tree came whooshing, and I threw myself to one side, rolled over several times and it was a close escape. Jesus, I thought, lying on my back in the grass and the sky above me was full of wind, was low and grey, but it did not matter now, I had done it, and I laughed, and I laughed all alone. Life lay ahead of me. Nothing was settled.

I stayed on my back to rest a bit until the cold seeped through my father's jumper. I listened for sounds from the house, but the house was quiet. No sounds from the kitchen. She had probably taken a sleeping pill. I sat up and pretended I was trying to decide whether I should cut the branches off at once. Or whether I should wait. I sat for a while in case there was someone watching me, before

195

I decided it could wait.

I got back on my feet, brushed dirt and pine needles off my jumper and off the seat of my trousers and went over to untie the rope from the trunk of the pine tree and pick up the tools I had used and carried everything back to the woodshed and leaned them against the wall, coiled the rope around my hand and elbow and finished it with a nice little knot before I hung it back on its hook, closed the door and crossed the grass towards the old shed.

Twilight would soon set in, the black autumn dark would roll in from the sea, the outer dark, so to speak, would come all the way from the horizon like a thick tarpaulin and blanket the coast and the beaches to the south and to the north and lie flat across the fields and the heath and every single road and every single path and then maybe weigh me down, so I would not be able to stand up straight.

But there were still some hours left. I opened the door to the shed and entered the familiar air of long-damp brickwork. I wanted to see if my old bicycle was still in there. And it was. Leaned up against the far wall. It was a Norwegian Svithun, metallic blue with white stripes. Both tyres were flat, but I found a rusty pump in a corner, and with some effort

I blew them both up, and they had no punctures, had merely been left unattended for so long the air had seeped out many years ago. I carried the bicycle on to the grass, pushed it along and swung myself up on the saddle. It felt like something I had never done, and the chain was rusty and noisy inside the shiny chain guard, but I gave it my best and tried to look swift on my way into town.

18

I cycled into town along the Skagen Road, pleased with myself and the pine tree that was lying across the yard in all its Danish majesty. I pedalled smoothly past the old DK petrol station where we so often had stopped to buy new stocks of beer when the other shops were shut. More than once I had come in my car, half drunk and parked so close to the petrol pump I could hardly get out.

And I cycled past the shop called Storkøb on my right and further along the long stone wall to the left, with Flagstrand church behind it, its whitewashed walls blinding in the late afternoon sunshine, and I free-wheeled along the cemetery that shared its tall trees with the small park, Plantagen, at the far end where they seamlessly merged. Halfway there I stopped and leaned my bike against the stone wall. There was only one other bike there, a ladies' bike, and I took my tobacco pouch out of my pocket and rolled a cigarette, and leaning against the wall I smoked the cigarette, holding it between my fingers like Albert Finney from the bicycle factory would have held his, had he been able

198

to travel through time to stand here in this place next to me. I looked up at the undertaker's across the street. A row of shiny, smooth, square gravestones was on display either side of the entrance, and bronze doves peered down from atop the stones in a modest and annoyingly Christian manner. I turned my head and looked down the road in the other direction, towards the hospital and the care home at the junction. It had balconies running all the way around the three floors. In a wicker chair my grand-mother had sat out the last years of her life before she finally was buried in the cemetery right behind me, and on one of the few occasions I had gone there to visit with one of the girls in tow, or with both of them, she had had a piece of paper in her lap where it said: *Arvid's coming today.* But she forgot about the piece of paper, and it lay loosely in her hand on the knitted blanket that was always draped across her knees, and she did not know who I was.

I didn't understand what it was about my body, if it was the cigarette I was smoking, if it had some narcotic effect, or it was the sunlight that still found its way over the rooftops, but I suddenly felt better than I had done for weeks. And as I was feeling so good, so high, even, I decided I might as well take a walk through the cemetery, among the trees, along the gravel paths while it was still light, because I liked that cemetery, I had walked there many times before.

The bare trees made it seem unfamiliar, and light was streaming through the branches, unlike in summer, when I would normally walk here, and you could see a long way even though the sun was setting. In the cemetery there were rows of neatly trimmed hedges, at strict angles around each grave, and chains were hanging between the path and the gravestone and some had small white painted cast iron gates in the low hedge, and more than half of the gravestones had doves on top of them, and one or two turned out to be real ones. As I walked by they spread their wings and flew off as doves do.

I knew where I was going, but I did not want to go there right away, so I turned left and walked onwards along the paths, and then approached the grave from a different direction than I usually did, this time facing the names carved into the stones, and that, of course, made the grave easier to find.

★ ★ ★

She was kneeling on the gravel in front of the gravestone with the three names on it, weeding, pulling twigs and dried dead flowers from the small pots she had placed there on her last visit. The time for flowers was long gone, but no one had been here for months to tend the grave. I stopped a few metres behind her and waited.

She did not turn around. 'Is that you?' she said.

'Yes,' I said, and she said nothing, so then I had to. 'I was certain you were asleep back in the summer house,' I said.

'As you can see, I'm not.'

'No,' I said. 'I can see that.'

I took a deep breath. I felt fine.

'Do you want a hand?' I said.

She half turned and looked up. She had been crying, it was clear to see.

'What happened to your forehead?' she said.

'I bumped into a tree,' I said.

'Just now?'

'Yes.'

'Were you drunk?'

'No,' I said. 'I don't get drunk on a glass of Calvados. And a beer.'

'A beer?'

'Yes, with Hansen.'

'I see,' she said. 'And what did the two of you talk about?'

'We talked about Lenin,' I said.

'Lenin?'

'Yes,' I said, and she shook her head and pointed past me along the path, and her face was swollen, the skin puffy under her eyes.

'You can fetch one of those buckets. By the door to the shed.'

I turned and looked in that direction. There was a pile of buckets at the door to a brick outhouse with a pointy roof of red tiles, and it looked nice in an old fashioned, slightly snobbish way.

There was a small concrete basin with a tap above it on the wall.

'Sure,' I said. 'Why not.' I walked the few metres and took a bucket from the top of the pile, went back and gave it to her. She placed it firmly between her knees and gathered the dead flowers and the twigs with her hands, and suddenly she stuffed it all violently into the bucket. She straightened up, took off her gloves and ran a hand through her hair and sat there in silence. It felt a little awkward so I decided to tell her now.

'I pulled that pine tree down,' I said, and at once I realised it was not the right time.

'Did you?'

'I sure did,' I said.

'That's good,' she said, 'but to be honest, you owe your father that much, he's not strong enough any more; he has done so

202

much for you,' she said, and I thought, what the hell has my father ever done for me? and she said: 'You're the strong one now. Your father is an old man. Do you understand that?'

'Yes, I understand,' I said.

'Are you sure?'

'Sure I'm sure. I understand that,' I said, 'but I didn't quite finish the job. So far the tree is just lying there. There are still the branches. That will take a while,' I said.

'Yes, of course,' she said, but she had already forgotten about the pine tree. I looked down at my shoes. 'Do you ever think of your brother?' she said.

'Yes,' I said, 'I do.'

'Every single day I think about him,' my mother said.

It was six years since he died, and I could not say the same. But I thought about him often, about the day he died and every single time with a guilty conscience. I had had that feeling for so long it was a part of who I was.

'You don't think about *me* every day,' I said.

'No,' she said. 'Why should I?'

'No, why should you,' I said. 'I don't think about you every day, either.' But that was not true, so I said: 'Yes, I do.'

'That's not necessary,' she said with her back to me.

'Yes, it is,' I said.

She turned and looked up into my eyes while at the same time pushing her bare hands against the gravel and got stiffly to her feet and was about to say something I was certain I would not like to hear, but then she let it go.

'It'll be dark soon,' she said. 'Shall we cycle home to the summer house together?' And I said:

'I was thinking of going into town.'

'Then I hope you've got lights on your bicycle.'

'Oh, yes, I have,' I said. And I did, but there was no dynamo. It was lost long ago and was probably on some other bicycle. Or just dumped somewhere. What did I know?

We walked together up to the gate. The cemetery was closing, a man in overalls came towards us. He nodded and my mother nodded back, and then we were outside and walked up to our bicycles.

'Very well,' she said and got on her bicycle seat, turning her back to me, and I climbed on to mine and we went our separate ways. When I reached the junction, I turned to the left before the care home and further down the road my chest started to hurt badly and I shouted:

'Fuck! Fuck!' and I could have flung my

old bicycle on the tarmac and ripped the saddle off the pole, twisted the handlebars into an 'S' with my hands and stamped the spokes around the hub into spaghetti, or turned around in the middle of the road and raced her to the petrol station and declaimed a sentence that would build a stunning bridge from my heart to hers. But I did none of those things. I just cycled down the street into town, across Gammeltorv, past Dommergaarden with the drunk tank to the right, where once I had been forced to stay the night, and after that I sailed across Nytorv and along the Danmarksgade, which was the main street in this town.

19

It was night on Carl Berners Plass. I was sleeping, I was dreaming, and then I woke up and forgot my dream. Cold it was against my face in the dark in the living room and I felt her body close to mine, and my chest was burning and my heart too, and a house somewhere in the city was burning, not far from this room. One man was shouting frightened words to another man who shouted back and both of them were panting, running as the fire engine howled past in the dark, crashing through red lights at the crossing where no one walked. I heard it all crashing through the open window in the cold, and the flashing blue lights hit the glass and were thrown back out, and it was burning down along my arm, around her shoulder and her arm around my chest was burning, and how strange it did not happen here, I thought, with the burning heat between her skin and my skin; how strange we did not burst into flames.

I remember getting up from the sofa and walking naked to the window, and it was cold December and snow on the bushes along the brick wall right below me and snow on the tarmac outside. I leaned out with the icy windowsill against my stomach, and it should have been a grey dawn now, almost morning, but the orange blue light I could see in the distance made everything around it look black.

'What's going on?' she said.

'There's a house on fire down the road somewhere,' I said, 'a tenement by the Munch Museum.'

'Oh, no,' she said, 'not the Munch Museum,' for we went there at least every other Sunday, stood waiting outside until the doors were opened.

'No, not that far down. The Munch Museum will be all right,' I said. 'But that house will not.'

She crossed the floor right behind me and we stood by the window shoulder to shoulder, she and I, and me with no clothes on and she wrapped in the warm duvet. In Finnmarkgata there were glowing circles on the snow below the street lamps, and the lights had come on in several flats across the road, and she said:

'But aren't you cold?' I shivered and said:

'Yes, I guess I am,' for I suddenly realised that I *was* freezing, like the naked sculptures in Frognerparken, glittering with hoar frost, in December, January, and then she opened the duvet and pulled me in, and we stood a while in our own warmth.

★ ★ ★

She tiptoed back to the sofa with the duvet tightly around her, and lay down and said:

'Please don't wake me again, I need my beauty sleep.'

'No problem,' I said, thinking: you couldn't be any prettier than this, and I closed the window and got dressed in a cold shirt and cold trousers, and barefoot I walked out into the kitchen with my socks and shoes in my hands, closed the door quietly, carefully behind me, and then she called out:

'Be my comrade and leave the door open, please,' so I opened the door and did not switch the light on and lifted the lid of the old cooker I had brought with me when I moved from Veitvet. I held my hands above the hotplate in the dark and rubbed them hard before I put the kettle on. Drops of water hissed under the kettle and cracked against the glowing cast iron, where heat rose from the filaments through the cylinder in a muted rumble, and the sound from the kettle was a fine sound, a sound I knew, a sound I had heard almost every morning standing on a stool with my hands outstretched half an hour on the dot after my father had caught the bus to the factory, and only she and I would be in the kitchen this early. Everyone else was asleep, it was dark outside in the street, dark inside the living room, only the yellow light on the cooker in the kitchen was lit, and there was a crack like airgun shots under the kettle when she heated milk to make cocoa. It was just she and I, for my brothers always slept late, my baby brother, my big brother, and they did not even know I was awake, that I had been lying in bed listening for the click of the door and my father's fading steps on the flagstones in front of the house. They did not know that I was waiting under the duvet, counting his long strides up the hill, past the red telephone booth, past the shopping centre, all the way up to Trondhjemsveien where the bus stopped that would take my father into town. Then I got up and dressed in the pitch dark, so the others would not see what I was doing if they suddenly woke up to go to the toilet. I tiptoed down the stairs to the living room and along the hall where my uncle from Denmark hung in a silver frame. His name was Jesper, and he wore a blue cap with stripes and a tassel and a Danish army uniform and died right after that photo was taken, only thirty-three years old, like Jesus was when he died.

And then I reached the kitchen and quietly stood on the threshold. She was standing in front of the cooker with her back to the door.

'Is that you?' she said.

'Yes,' I said, 'it's me,' and every single time she knew that it was me, every single time she knew that it was me who stood there, even though I came barefoot and noiseless when I came, like a Kiowa through the woods, I was mysterious and dark, and she said:

'Can't you sleep?' and I said:

'No, you know I can't,' and then she almost certainly smiled to herself before turning around, and she turned around and was not smiling very much, not really smiling, but nor was she displeased for she knew that it was me coming. She took the stool from under the kitchen counter and placed it in front of the cooker and bent down to get the milk from the bottom shelf of the cupboard by the hatch that was covered with mesh to keep the mice out. I climbed on to the stool, knees first, then stood with my arms outstretched over the open hotplate to feel the shimmering heat seep up along my hands, along my chest, all the way up to my chin and my mouth, and the kettle banged on the hotplate and I had not even started school yet, so I could stand there for as long as I wanted.

*   *   *

I sat down at the table with the hot coffee in a pale yellow mug and thought about the burning building down the road and the people living in the flats that were burning, waking up in the middle of the night with the red hot air around them, running with their children in their arms, down the stairs to the ground floor, and at the last minute stumbling into cold December, and the cold felt like a shock to their faces. But everything that must be done was done by those who knew how, and I did not want to go out to stand there staring like the others and be one of them. And I had to get going, it would soon be six o'clock. I closed the lid of the hotplate, and made myself a packed lunch and put it in a bag, which looked like the bag my father always carried, a leather bag with one big compartment containing my lunch and copies of *Arbeiderbladet* and *Klassekampen*, folded so the logo could not be seen, and two pockets at the front with my notebook and my pen and the latest resolutions from the Party leadership, as well as the book I was reading at the time.

I went into the living room to watch her sleep in the grey, muted, slanted light from the window. I stood there and did not say anything that might wake her, because soon she would have to get up and go to school in town. Sometimes when she was asleep and I was awake I felt a little uneasy, for she looked so young on the pillow, only a girl, and I thought, she is so young, and in her sleep she had whispered: Oh, Arvid, from her floating state between here and there, and no embarrassing slip did she make in the dark, no other name rose from some previous embrace, no Gunnar, no Espen, no Tommy, no, certainly no Tommy, but Arvid, only Arvid; for he who bore the name Arvid was the first, was the one who held it all in his hands, held everything in balance, and sometimes when these thoughts came over me, I found it hard to bear. She did not feel young, she said, and she did not feel young to me, not young in that way, she knew things that I did not, but she *was* young. It troubled me sometimes.

★　★　★

I felt her warmth and the warmth from the stove still inside me, it was early morning on Carl Berners Plass. I crossed the tramlines, cut my way beneath the cables that powered the trams and the neon signs were not yet switched on, and it felt right that they were not; half blinded you embraced your own body, and with the warmth still under your jacket, you walked up the pavement along the square, moving through the grey light, and let your thoughts seep softly in, undisturbed, on the way up to the station, but also walking as one of many in the chill of December. I liked the feeling of being a we, being more than myself, being larger than myself, being surrounded by others in a way I had never experienced before, of belonging, and it made no difference if those who walked to the left or the right of me, in front or behind me on this street, did not share the same feeling. We were the proletariat on our way to the Underground station, to the places where we toiled, and everyone in the Party was annoyed because I often said the *peuple* rather than the working class. It was an anachronism, it was just nonsense, they said, but I would never stop saying that, it felt right to me in a way they did not understand. None of them had read Victor Hugo, they only read what was in front of them, they did not know that what had failed in the revolutionary years of 1830, 1848, 1871, was what we were going to achieve, once and for all, and in my bag I had the latest resolutions from the Party's leadership. I knew well that I would never be able to carry them through, in fact I did not carry much through, I was too shy, I was too alone, I had my back against the wall, I did not want to be alone, but it did not matter just now, in the half-dark on the way to the Underground station, whether I knew that I would succeed or not. Everyone around me knew so much more than me anyway, all the women around me, all the men. I knew too little. And still there was nothing I wanted more than to walk here, towards the station in the grey light and be surrounded by them all.

★ ★ ★

Past the loading ramp, through the plastic double-doors, cold outside, warm inside, the forklift trucks parked along the wall. The concourse was quiet and there was a freshness to the air you did not normally feel in here between the machines, no dull blows against your earmuffs, no whirls of dust in your eyes, no heat, no smell of burnt plastic from the melting chamber, no hum from the assembly lines, or itching or sticky sweat. The old-timers in their blue work clothes hung around the coffee machine, small-talking about things of no consequence, and Elly, sleepy Elly so remote in her pale blue apron, standing there, or sometimes sitting, five pallets up dangling her legs. No one was called Elly any more, except Elly. She had nice legs. She was ten years older than me, perhaps more, and I guess it showed, but it was hard not to look at her. She smiled to me above the shoulders of the old men, and she winked, and I winked back and walked the stairs down to the basement and the locker rooms where at last I had been given one, after someone had left. Having your own locker was important. You could hold your head high.

★   ★   ★

Two hours into the shift the foreman came over. The air was thick with dust, every machine was rolling, the small one and the two big ones and I was standing at one of them and time after time I had to run to the forklift truck to bring forward new pallets with seven stacks of paper so the belt would not stop. The A team was doing well even though two of us were off work that day. I removed my earmuffs, bent down and turned my naked ear to the foreman's mouth and he told me I had to go and see the personnel director. Now. He looked at me and left. I

215

looked down the belt, along the platform we were standing on, feeding our stations, Elly and Reidun and Reidar and I, and I waved to Hassan who was running the machine and pointed to my chest and then to the door leading through to the office block. I filled my stations elegantly with thirty-two pages of folded, hard fibre, porous paper manufactured in Norway by Follum Factories. Hassan came over. He showed me five stiff fingers on his right hand and counted them one after the other with the index finger of his left hand, right in front of my face to make sure I got everything right. I nodded, and he smiled, and as everything was running smoothly, he took over my station. Hassan was all right. I stepped down from the platform and walked through the concourse and out through the soundproof door to the part of the business that had carpets on the floors and potted plants by the lift.

Four floors up. It just said *Tommy* on the door, suggesting he was one of the boys, was one of us all in every department and to give the door an intimacy I was not sure I liked. I did not like it. I knocked on the door and entered.

'Yes?' I said.

'Hello,' he said. 'Just a moment.'

I stood there waiting for several minutes.

Was he trying to psych me out, I wondered, make me look like an idiot, make me feel less than I was? I grew uncertain. Not scared, but uncertain. Perhaps he knew something I did not, something that could harm me? If that was the point he was doing a good job, but he didn't know that. I smiled vaguely the whole time, and then he raised his head and said:

'Do you know why we gave you a job here?'

'Because I applied, I suppose.'

'Because your father called to ask if we would. Give you a job.'

'I see,' I said.

'We liked your father here. He gave his all, every single shift, he was never ill, never caused any trouble. It was not his fault that the shifts and the overtime became too much for him. He's not a young man any more.'

'I know,' I said.

'That was the only reason.'

'I see,' I said.

'Yes, that was all.'

I turned and headed for the door, and when I got there and had my hand on the door handle, I stopped and said:

'Do you know who the *peuple* is?'

'I don't give a shit.'

'I thought so,' I said with something that was meant to be a sarcastic smile, but it was clear that he did not give a damn about the *peuple*, nor why I asked the question, and anyway he was already looking at his papers again and did not see my smile. And I thought, am I a man who could step forward and kick the personnel director called Tommy so hard on the shin he would be forced to give me the sack, and yet leave the factory with my head held high? But I knew that I was not, and on my way down in the lift from the fourth floor I was gasping for air.

20

I did not understand. It felt so long since I walked down the gangplank of the *Holger Danske* and into this town, and it was early morning. This day. It should have been over by now. It was November, it was evening, it should have been dark, but the sun was still hanging low above the rooftops to the west, where it glowed faintly and refused to let go.

I cycled past the Palads Theatre in the far north of the town. In front of the old cinema there were long shadows falling in razor sharp lines across the houses on the opposite side, but they were not long enough, not dark enough to soften this angular, insistent light.

At a kiosk that was still open, there were newspapers stacked on a stand outside, and in large bold typeface on every front page it said THE WALL TUMBLES, and I could not breathe, where had I been? This was bad, I had not paid attention, it was really bad, and I started to cry. I felt my tears flow right through town from Gammeltorv, and they flowed across the junction with the Løve Pharmacy and then down across the square by the Svane Pharmacy. Time had passed behind my back and I had not turned to look, that was really, really bad, and I cycled on with tears flowing down my face along Søndergade all the way to the south of town, to a place where I used to drink beer in the olden days. It was almost as far as Møllehuset and the mill brook and the ice cream stall that was closed now, like everything else was closed, and all the way out to the Bangsbo Manor park with its two golden tigers which everyone thought were lions resting on plinths to either side of the entrance. The manor was a museum now and had been for many years. I had gone there several times with the girls. It was a good museum. We entered the big, horseshoe-shaped main building to look at the exhibits from places around the town and from the coast and inland, and there was furniture a hundred years old or even more, and clothes with lace and wide shirt fronts, and work clothes and vast numbers of photographs in off white and sepia on the walls. On the way out we bought lollies from the counter and stood on the white painted bridge across the moat and fed stale bread to the ducks from a bag we had brought with us. We broke the bread into suitable chunks and threw them into the water one by one, and the ducks came swimming at full speed from all directions in a splash of foam, flapping to get there ahead of each other in a whirling chaos, and sometimes the carp would come darting, straight out of nowhere, their backs red, and would get there first and drag the pieces of bread down into the tea-coloured water and disappear towards the bottom.

★ ★ ★

I made a turn towards the manor park and wiped my face, that was cold now in the cold wind and clammy against my palms, but the tears were no longer running from my eyes and I thought of all the photographs from Berlin I had seen, and especially the one with the soldier in his shiny helmet and spotless uniform floating across the no man's land between East and West, his gun on his back, muzzle down, stock up, hanging there suspended in the air with the coiled barbed wire beneath him for almost thirty years, and wondered if he finally was allowed to land now.

★ ★ ★

With the bicycle between my legs I stood for a while gazing past the towering ash and chestnut trees and beeches towards the large, white house at the far end of the park; the white bridge, everything bare now, unflowering, pure and clean. Only one man was wandering along the footpaths with burlap sacks under his arm covering the pruned flowers that would die when the frost came. If it came.

Then I turned the bicycle around and went back a bit the same way I had come, up Søndergade to the place where I used to drink when the wall was still standing, but when I got there, I could not find it. I pushed the bicycle along the building. There was the usual second-hand furniture, clothes and the unloved books for sale in the Santal Mission charity shop, and to the right of its large windows was the door I could have sworn led to the bar where I had planned to have a beer. But there was not even a sign with CLOSED hung up behind the glass or *Moved to this* or *that* address. The café was simply gone. Above the window it said FONA in hard blue neon lights. I shielded my eyes with both hands and leaned towards the window and peered through the glass, and inside there were rows of television sets and stereos for sale.

'Goddamnit,' I said out loud, and suddenly the urge for a beer was stronger than usual. There was a fissure in my life, a void, and that void, only beer could fill.

A man passed me on the pavement. He had probably heard me swearing and walked on in a strange and cautious way to a door a bit further down in the next house. Almost always there were white pots with red geraniums on a windowsill if it was an apartment. And sure enough, there they were, the geraniums, and the man pulled a key out of his pocket, but then he turned and looked my way, and walked back when he realised why I was standing there and could see from my blue bicycle that I was not Danish, for all Danish bicycles are black.

'You haven't been here for a while,' he said in a kind of Swedish. 'They closed two years ago,' and I thought why the hell is it that all Danes think that all Norwegians are Swedes and at the same time speak such dreadful Swedish? We are three countries in Scandinavia, for Christ's sake.

'They've moved,' he said and pointed back into town. 'They're next to Rose's Bookshop.' As though everyone knew where Rose's Bookshop was. But *I* knew where Rose's Bookshop was. I had cycled there from the summer house through town when I was a youngster, and younger even, and had stood outside to gaze at the new books in the window and leafed through the remainder boxes on the pavement outside the shop and always found something I wanted, that I could afford.

'Thank you,' I said. 'Then I'll go back to the bar next door to Rose's Bookshop and get drunk.'

'You're not Swedish,' he said. 'You're Norwegian.'

'Not bad,' I said. 'Really, not bad at all. Then perhaps not so very drunk,' I said.

'I hope not,' he said.

'Again, thank you very much,' I said, and got on my bicycle.

'Good luck,' he said.

★　★　★

First, I stopped outside the bookshop. It was late in the day, there was a grille outside the door, but the obstinate light still stayed in the sky, and the lamps in the ceiling above the window display were lit. Klaus Rifbjerg had a new book out. He had almost every year. And there was a collected edition of la Cour's poems. And a paperback edition of *Hærværk* (*Ravaged*) by Tom Kristensen, about the alcoholic journalist and critic, Ole Jastrau. That book terrified me so the first time I read it that I promised myself and the god who did not exist that I would never ever touch alcohol. Then I parked my bike in a cycle stand and entered the bar.

Inside it was brown and gloomy. The first thing I saw through the haze of tobacco smoke was the illuminated bar and the men with their elbows on the counter between all kinds of bottles, and little by little more men and a few women emerged in the booths to the right and the left of me. They were all drinking beer and smoking cigarettes, Prince, I supposed, and they spoke about things they knew something about, but that were alien to me, and in here they could keep each other informed by exchanging views on the most recent progress in any topic worth talking about, like the need for icebreakers in a time like ours when the ice no longer lay that solid, about shipbuilding, the size of the gas tankers owned by the Alpha Diesel company, and most certainly they talked about the Wall which, to my total surprise, had fallen, hurling chunks of concrete to East and West, and every sound from every corner of the room was deafening, almost menacing after the silence of the street. But when I came down the steps the room went quiet. Everyone turned and looked at me. I walked quietly up to the bar, the last few paces maybe less confident than the first, and found the only available space between the men standing there. They all had one elbow resting on the counter, and were all facing me.

I ordered a beer and said:

'Draught beer, please, if you have any.' I could see nothing but bottles scattered along the counter, bottles of Carlsberg and Tuborg, but I did not feel like bottled beer. It was too lukewarm and there was not enough of it.

Draught beer was no problem. The barman took a glass, pulled the handle and filled it and there was too much foam so he scraped the foam off the glass with a wooden spatula and filled the glass to the brim a second time and placed it in front of me on a beer mat, which said Carlsberg in green and white letters with a red crown in the middle.

The men started talking again, and the few women too. At first just barely audible, and then louder and louder until they were almost back at the volume they had when I entered the room, but not quite, and perhaps a little more guarded, a little more private, as if I were an informer for the shipyard, where I guessed most of them worked.

I took a deep swig of my beer, and it really did taste good, so I took another and put the glass back on its Carlsberg beer mat and gave a sigh, that could be heard by many, and rolled a cigarette with tobacco from my Petterøe 3 tobacco pouch, and lit it with the blue lighter. The man that was second closest to me along the counter leaned across the man beside me and looked at my tobacco pouch and said:

'So you're Norwegian.'

'Yes,' I said, 'that's right.' And I thought, what is it about this day that I keep bumping into Danes who have such a profound insight into the field of Scandinavian languages?

'Pardon me for asking, but, eh, in that case what are you doing here?'

'I am here to drink beer,' I said.

'Eh, I can see that, but, eh, there are other places in town where you can drink beer. So why this place? You don't know anyone in here, eh, isn't that right?'

'That's quite right,' I said, and thought he really said *ch* a lot.

'So why here?'

'This is my town,' I said. 'I drink beer wherever I want,' and then suddenly I felt untouchable. I turned my body all the way round and with my back against the bar, I faced the room. I was a man that no one could harm. It was not true, but the people in the bar didn't know that.

'Eh,' he said. 'Your town?'

'I more or less grew up in this town, as a matter of fact.'

'But, eh, you don't speak Danish.'

'No, I don't. But that doesn't mean you can't understand what I'm saying.'

'Most Danes mistake Norwegians for, eh, Swedes. They, eh, can't hear the difference.'

'That's it. It's fucking irritating,' I said, and thought how irritating it was that he kept saying *eh*. I took another deep swig of my beer and then the beer was gone. I raised my glass so the man behind the bar could see it and said:

'Another one, if I may.'

'You may,' he said. And I did. That pint and then some, and when I had drained my fourth, I was fairly drunk. I did not feel well at all. My head was spinning. I stood holding my fifth glass, raised it to my mouth and took a big swig and thought I had better leave, if I take just one more swig, I'm a goner. So I took another swig and a man in the furthest, darkest corner of the room stood up from his table and started walking towards me. His walk was not steady. Zombie-like he came into the light from the bar and his whole face was visible, and there was a purple and swollen mark across his left cheek, right above his cheekbone. I could not believe it. It was the man from the ferry. And he was still coming towards me. I did not know what to do, I got scared, I felt threatened, in fact I feared for my life. I squeezed my glass hard,

228

and then he stopped only a metre from me. He stood there, he said nothing, he blinked a few times, closed his eyes tightly shut, opened them again and looked into mine and said in a voice of such despair that I felt like crying:

'But why did you have to hit me?'

I took a deep breath, I did not defend my behaviour, I said: 'I'm truly sorry, I really am. I thought you were coming at me,' I said, 'that you wanted to hurt me.' And now I must have been drunk, no doubt about it, because I said: 'I was afraid you were going to throw me overboard.'

'What,' he said, 'throw you overboard?' And now he looked really baffled, and I felt sorry for him then, and not because of the swollen purple bruise on his cheek.

'I'm sorry,' I said again, 'it was unbelievably stupid of me to think that, but I did, I was a little drunk, you see, I got scared.'

'Scared of me? But it's me, Mogens.'

'What?' I said.

'It's Mogens,' he said. 'My name's Mogens.'

'Mogens,' I said.

'I'm Mogens. Your friend. You shouldn't hit your friends. It's not right.'

'We're friends?' I said. He was drunker than I'd realised. He was drunker than me.

'Of course, we're friends. Don't you

remember anything? I recognised you at once when I saw you on the ferry,' said the man called Mogens in a trembling voice, but now with a sudden undertone of anger.

I did not understand. He had recognised me on board the ferry, in the bar of the *Holger Danske*, how could he recognise me in the bar of the *Holger Danske*? It's Mogens, I thought, his name is Mogens, Jesus, it is Mogens. I had known only one Mogens in my life, and he had been my friend, that was true. And suddenly it was plain to see it was Mogens standing in front of me, he had just grown older as I had grown older, and I had been so wrong when I told myself in the bar of the *Holger Danske* last evening or last night, that the man at the other end of the room could not possibly know anything about my life, because Mogens had been my friend. He had been my friend for years. Every single summer when I came down on ferries called the *Vistula* or the *Crown Prince Olav* or the *Skipper Clement* or the *Akershus*, or ferries with other names such as the *Cort Adeler* or the *Peter Wessel*, he would be standing at the terminal on the quay waiting and waving with his eyes fixed on the railing where I was leaning out far too far, waving back. I had never understood how he could have known which day we would arrive. Still, whenever we docked with one ferry or another, no matter what that ferry was called, he stood waiting by the green terminal, and right then and there in the bar next to Rose's Bookshop, in 1989, I realised he had gone to the quay every single morning for a week, or maybe longer, to wait in case I did arrive that very day on the big ferry and would see him standing by the green terminal building and raise my hand to wave.

I tried hard to stand without swaying. I held out my right hand.

'Hi, Mogens,' I said, 'it's been a long time. Really good to see you again.' And he took my hand and squeezed it hard, and said:

'Oh, you think so,' and punched me on the cheek with his left fist while still holding my right hand with his right hand, so I didn't fall far when I fell, but was dangling from his arm and he hit me again, and he opened his hand and let me fall to the floor between the legs of the men by the bar. Jesus Christ, that hurt. I closed my eyes and lay flat on my back, and my cheek really hurt, I could not recall such pain, and not one man at the bar helped me up. I hoisted myself on to my elbows and watched Mogens turn and walk very slowly back to the table in the deepest, darkest corner. Our friendship was over, and at once I began to miss it, the way it once was, the way it could have been, but all the summers were gone, and not only because I had forgotten them after twenty-five years, but because there was no longer any point remembering them.

21

It would be Christmas soon. I had stood at
the machine for six months, and all this time
I had tried to carry out every single Party
resolution, but I had not succeeded. I had
run for a seat on the local union board and
received four votes; two from old friends of
my father's, who felt they had to. I had Elly's
vote, and the man who swept the floors gave
me *his* vote, because he was hard of hearing
and had raised his hand at the wrong time.
They called me Little Stalin, but I had never
said anything about Stalin, I hated Stalin, he
had ruined everything.

But the work itself was going well, that was
the weird thing. I was no worse than the
others, but rather the swiftest on the A team,
the most accurate, everything I did on that
floor came easy to me. I found pleasure in
most of it, I liked the rhythm of the belt, the
sharp smell from the melting chamber, driving the forklift through the door to the ramp
with pallets of shrink-wrapped magazines twelve
layers high and turning on a sixpence towards
the rear end of the lorry and lowering the
pallets slowly within a centimetre and sliding

out again to get the next.

Those I knew from the college in Dælenenggata said I was brave, but also said that the work I was doing was boring and might damage the brain the way I had to perform the same movements over and over again every single day for the rest of my life, but, to tell the truth, I did not mind. It came as a surprise, even to me, that the work left me free to ponder all sorts of things I felt were important, or I could just dream myself away when the noise was at its loudest. The work was not difficult, but it required precision and rhythm and a will to collaborate with other bodies, and I had that will, and I enjoyed the feeling of rushing around the factory concourse to find a mechanic or take the goods lift down to the print works, or just standing at the belt next to Elly when everything ran like clockwork, and in the few minutes' break, turning the page in the book I was reading at the time, *The Myth of Wu Tao-tzu* by Sven Lindqvist, where at the end it says:

Is social and economic liberation possible without violence? No. Is it possible with violence? No.

It was something to think about, and I did, as the days passed one after the other, and yet it did not turn out as I had hoped it would.

There was a void between me and the other workers in the hall, and every single time I tried to turn the conversation from football to the factions in the trade union movement — the red, revolutionary, and the blue, conservative — they would simply pat me on the shoulder, laugh and walk away, to sit on a pallet and smoke cigarettes when there was a short break, or laugh all the way up the stairs to the canteen to play a game of cards at lunchtime. And even though my father had been there for many years and was liked by everyone and everyone had told me how I looked just like him, I did not *want* to be like him, did not want to enjoy my work as he had enjoyed his. I did not feel like him, I never had. I wanted to be different. I wanted to make a difference. But I did not, and it suddenly dawned on me that what I had tried to do might not be possible: to leave behind the Arvid I had been up to this point in life, to pull him up by his hair and then lower him into some other Arvid I still did not know, yes, with full conviction turn my back on the Arvid who was loved by those he loved the most, who greeted him and called him by pet names when he passed them in front of the house, the Arvid who got one hundred kroner notes from his mother when he was broke, but now had done what *I* had done and joined the *peuple* which really did not exist any more, but was an anachronism. I was a man out of time, or my character had a flaw, a crack in its foundation that would grow wider with each year.

* * *

And then there was a double shift, the evening shift and overtime until the morning, and it was starting to wear me down. I was confused, I felt cheated. I took the Underground home and then we had to wait at Hasle Station because a man collapsed in the aisle. He thrashed about with his arms and legs, epilepsy I guessed it was. I had not seen a fit like that before. His head was pounding the floor and the people in the carriage were so tired they did not know what to do or did not want to be hauled out of their sleepy bubble, and so they sat there, mute and awkward, and it fell to me to snap out of *my* bubble into the garish life outside and order someone to hold him fast so he would not beat himself senseless against the pole or the door. And it was I who ran through the carriages to alert the train driver, because I was a Communist or a Boy Scout, one of those things, but it turned out all right in the end, and I got off the train at the blue station and walked up the incline and out through the revolving doors with a windmill in my head. It was morning and there was a bite in the air I was not used to, a constant, artificial light blinding my eyes. I had started to squint and wore sunglasses in all weathers, there was a sore spot in my throat that would not heal, a raw patch, like an infection.

★   ★   ★

The station doors slammed behind me, and suddenly there was Elly walking up Grenseveien from Carl Berners Plass in a light-coloured coat, a blue leather bag slung over her shoulder, a cigarette between her fingers. We almost crashed into each other. She stopped and I stopped, and there was only a metre between us. Seeing her in other clothes than the blue work apron made me feel shy, she looked alien and feminine in a bewildering way. I was blushing, I could feel it, and she said:

'Hi there, Arvid. So you're standing here looking good?'

I caught the scent of her perfume on the wintry air, and the perfume was probably a little on the strong side, but it certainly hit me in the gut in a way, I suppose, is the whole point of perfume.

'Actually I am on my way home to get some sleep, I've worked the double shift, yesterday evening and all night.' I wanted to tell her about the man who had a fit and collapsed in the carriage, but I did not have the energy.

'I bet your head is spinning,' she said, and I said that it was, and then I said:

'But you don't take the train from Carl Berners Plass, do you?'

'I have moved,' she said, 'that's why I'm running a bit late too. The man I used to live with, let's not talk about him, the bloody idiot. Now I have a flat close by the Munch Museum, right across Tøyenparken, so I guess I could walk to Tøyen Station as well. You really should come and visit me, now that we live so close,' she said, 'we could have a great time.' She smiled.

'Yes, sure, that would be great,' I said, and I did not know whether I could visit her, I did not think so, still she told me her address.

'I'll never be able to remember that,' I said.

'All right, hang on a moment,' she said and rummaged around in the blue bag until she found a used envelope and a pen, and she was nearly forty years old, and I was just over twenty.

'Turn around,' she said, and smiled, 'and lean forwards.' I turned and leaned forwards, and then she wrote her address very slowly on the envelope against my back, and her perfume hit me stronger now, and her hands on my back made the sore spot in my throat feel even worse, and it was soft too, the way she touched me, and I thought maybe I was going to cry. But I was not, and Elly put the envelope with her street and house number written on it into the pocket of my jacket, gently, still standing behind me, leaning over me, and she gave me a hug, from behind, and I felt her mouth against my ear and the scent of her perfume and her body all the way down in the unfamiliar, light-coloured coat, and my head filled with shapeless, wild thoughts.

★ ★ ★

I came home, walked to the kitchen, took the juice from the fridge and, leaning against the kitchen counter, I drank a big glass and went into the living room and pulled the bed linen out from behind the sofa and lay down under the duvet and stayed there staring at the ceiling. I tried to collect all that was in my head into one straight line.

★ ★ ★

I slept until late in the afternoon and was still lying on the sofa bed when she came back from school on the tram. She let herself in, and I heard her take off her coat, her scarf and mittens in the hall. My clothes were already hanging there, so she could see that I was home, but she just went on into the kitchen like a grown woman would, with her regular habits after many years in the same flat, and filled the kettle and put it on the stove. I heard the drops of water hiss against the hotplate. She always made tea when she came home from school, and she no longer had to throw up in the morning and only went to see her parents a couple of times a week. Perhaps this was home to her now. Then she pulled her books out of her satchel and put them on the kitchen table and spent an hour or more doing her homework, and I was lying dozily expectant in the living room, and then she came in and lay down next to me under the duvet, and afterwards we sat on the sofa bed with the duvet wrapped around us as we always sat, and it was evening still, it was dark early as always in December, but not completely dark. I smoked a cigarette, and the tip glowed, and the grey and white smoke coiled almost invisibly above our heads before it was carried off by the draught along the wall and out through the open window to

240

Finnmarkgata. Outside the traffic was still rushing past in both directions, and the lights from the cars reflected in the double-glazed windows and swept past Mao and all the way in to the sofa. At the junction the traffic lights changed from green to amber to a painful red and back again. We sat warm and our skin was gleaming, and I always imagined that if anyone saw us sitting like this, they would see something they could never have, something absent from their lives, and then that would be like a thorn in their side.

I passed her the cigarette, but she did not take it. I turned. She was staring down at the duvet.

'Hi,' I said.

'Hi,' she said.

'Is something wrong?' I said.

'No.'

'You sure?'

'You were different this time,' she said.

'Different how?' I said.

'I don't know. Just different.'

'Wasn't it good, didn't you feel good?'

'Yes,' she said.

'Well, that's all right, isn't it?'

'I guess so,' she said and bit her lip and stared down at the duvet and she was crying. Perhaps she had been crying all the time we were lying next to each other, and I had not noticed. I put my arm around her shoulder and pulled her to me.

'But it's just you and me,' I said, 'just you and me, and we do things that no one else could know about, and they ache to know and then they feel sad, because they long to feel the way we feel, but they cannot. They know nothing. Only you and I can feel this way,' and her arms hung limply as I squeezed her tight. She did not put them around my shoulders, nor did she lay her hands where she always laid them. She cried and said:

'But it didn't feel like that. It felt as though everyone could see what we were doing. That it wasn't only us.'

I did not know what to say. I let go of her and took the last drag from the cigarette and leaned forwards and stubbed it out in the ashtray between the piles of books on the table. I stroked her back.

'Did you go home last night?' I said. I knew she had.

'Yes,' she said.

'Was it bad?'

'Yes, it was.'

'Perhaps you're just tired,' I said, 'why don't you sleep a little, it doesn't matter if it's still early, wouldn't that be all right? Do you have homework?'

'I did it when I got here. There's just a little

bit left and I can do it behind the library tomorrow morning. It's not very cold either.'

'There you go. So why don't you sleep then?'

'I am a bit tired.'

'I will lie down here beside you. I don't have to go to a meeting or anything.'

'Oh, that's good,' she said, and we lay down, and I pulled the duvet over her and held her tight until she was asleep, and then I stood up and went naked out into the kitchen and sat down at the table and rolled another cigarette. I was cold next to the window and I lit my cigarette with a match my fingers could barely hold. I did not understand how she could feel that I had been thinking of someone else.

22

The sound of a car woke me up. I did not know where I was, if it was day or night. I had no name, no home in time. I could have been twelve, I could have been sixty-eight. I opened my eyes and stared straight up at the bunk above me and I remembered that bunk from all the years and my own life and the night before in every detail, and then I was back in the summer house with a bang. But it didn't feel right, and it was as though something different, more appropriate, more flattering for my person was gone with sleep.

I heard the car stop with its engine still running and then someone turned the key and it fell silent. When I raised my head from the pillow and with great effort leaned towards the window and looked outside, I could see that it was a taxi. Grey dawn was in the air, like powder, like pepper, black and grey, and the paintwork of the car was black with its doors facing the summer house, so it could have been any car, but it was still an Audi, definitely an Audi, and the light on the roof was off. A young taxi driver climbed out and walked around the car and up towards the summer house. He stepped over two pine branches keeled over and my bicycle slumped against the trunk. He headed for the terrace, and then I could not see him. I had no idea what he was doing here. I swung out of the bottom bunk in some haste, and Jesus, how my head ached, oh Christ how my head ached, too many pints, no doubt about it. I touched my cheek, and it was throbbing in there, the gristle and bone, and I took my trousers from the back of the chair at the end of the bed, and my vest I took, and the charcoal jumper with the red trimming that once had belonged to my father and still did, I mean, he was not dead or anything, and I bundled the clothes under my arm and stormed out into the hall, and one of my brother's paintings hung on a nail to the right of the toilet door, and in that painting was a beach bathed in orange morning light and a bit of the island of Læsø to the east if you looked closely, and there was Hirsholmen on the horizon, its lighthouse pointing to the sky. I hobbled past the kitchen and into the living room. There I found my mother standing, fully dressed before the mirror, in a blue jacket with white flowers and navy blue trousers, her freshly washed hair and her curls rippling on her head. With one hand she was applying red lipstick, in the other she held a blue handbag; over her arm was her coat. It was pale, cream, almost white. On the floor was a blue canvas bag. Short boots with a zip. But her eyes were strangely narrow, as if that was the only way she could face the mirror.

The taxi driver was waiting outside on the terrace. Hansen stood there with the light from the living room window falling against his thigh, his elbow, the one side of his face lit up as if by a campfire, that kind of glow, and the other side so differently; the grey, peppery light from the sky. The driver must have been in his early twenties. They smiled to each other, laughed and talked with both hands in their pockets. Perhaps they knew each other, Hansen and the taxi driver. It was a small town. Hansen was dressed up too, in a dark jacket and pale trousers, an unfamiliar sight, as though he was going somewhere smart, a wedding or birthday party. I had never seen him looking so well dressed. What little hair he had left was combed across his head, there were curls at the back of his neck, and the jacket held his stomach in place.

'Are you going somewhere?' I said, 'now? What time is it? Are you going with Hansen?'

'We didn't want to wake you,' my mother said. 'You were so fast asleep.'

'We? What do you mean, we?' I said. 'Of course you should have woken me,' I said.

'You can't leave like this. Shouldn't we talk about it first?'

'There are things I have to do,' she said, 'and there isn't really that much to talk about. It is nothing very complicated. What happened to your cheek?'

'Nothing,' I said, 'it doesn't even hurt,' but it did, it hurt like hell. 'With Hansen,' I said. 'Have you talked with Hansen about it? And what about me?'

'What about you,' my mother said.

I took a deep breath. I looked at her.

'But you can't leave me here alone,' I said.

I could hear my own voice. It was embarrassing, as if it was coming from a different place entirely, from some other time, it sounded so childish, so whiny, it was thinner and more shrill than before. I happen to have a rich voice, I know that for a fact, but there was nothing I could do about it. It just kept going. It was like a jolt to my stomach. An electrical current. If I touched my skin, above my navel, it was ouch, ouch, that would hurt.

'We'll be away for a couple of days only.'

'I'm coming with you,' I said.

'You're thirty-seven years old, Arvid.'

'What's that got to do with anything?' I said, and I stood there, practically naked, cradling the bundle of clothes in my arms and my knees knocking against each another.

'Just give me a minute,' I said, 'and I'll be there.' And I ran back and saw her note in the middle of the table, and I ran to the tiny bathroom with my father's clothes in my arms and threw them in a pile on the toilet seat and splashed water on my face, splashed water in my armpits and water in my hair and pulled my hair back as hard as I could and tried not to look at my face in the mirror. I found a deodorant which my father had left behind when he was here last, Old Spice, it was, swirling white letters on the red surface, and the scent of it matched the clothes, no doubt about it, and two painkillers I took from a box I found, and with my mouth to the tap I swallowed them both, and the tap had a sharp metallic taste, and it was a bit too much, to tell the truth. My stomach churned and I brushed my teeth while I tried to think about something else.

I got dressed and went back to the living room. I saw my mother on the terrace, she shook the taxi driver's hand, and he smiled, happy as a puppy, and then she raised her arms in a gesture of resignation. And Hansen smiled a wry smile too, but I did not care. I did not want to be left alone.

I took my reefer jacket from the peg by the door, pulled it on over my father's worn clothes, and the jacket was not that clean any more, so I brushed it at the front and rubbed my hand across the creases and did up the double row of brass buttons, each with an anchor moulded into the metal, and then the boots with their laces. It went well, all things considered, and in a sudden flash of inspiration I ran to the kitchen counter where the bottle of Calvados still stood. It looked full, almost untouched, which was strange, but I opened my jacket and slipped the slim bottle into the inside spacious pocket. Then at last I could walk to the door and join the others.

'Let's be off then,' I said.

★ ★ ★

They put me in the front seat, next to the driver, and the driver was not too happy about that, he would rather have had my mother beside him. But there was nothing he could do about it. I didn't care where I sat. I did not even look at him. I leaned back in my seat and felt overcome by fatigue. We pulled out and drove down the road, and there was Mrs Kaspersen coming in the opposite direction on her black contraption on the way to her summer house. She turned and stared into the car and she must have seen who we were but she didn't greet us. It looked like she was crying.

Inside the car it was dark and quiet. No one said anything. I closed my eyes. Woolly grey sounds came seeping in from the air around us and damp sounds from the beach. A mute humming sound came from the tarmac, quivering up through my legs, through my stomach, and surrounded by it all I fell asleep, and when I opened my eyes, the car was standing still. My head no longer hurt. To my left the lamps at the shipyard were lit and floodlights hit the hull of a ship with the DFDS logo on the funnel, and the last remaining shadows were cut through by shafts of light from the welding torches working down the seams of the rust-coloured sheets of steel. At the far end of the harbour a boat was coming in from the sea through the gap in the breakwater, her blue bow high, the stern low, her lanterns still lit, and she looked like a fishing boat, one of the few then, out of this harbour. It was dawn, almost day. To my right a ferry was docked at the quay. Not as big as the ferries that sailed from this town to Oslo, Gothenberg. It said F/L in blue on the yellow funnel, so then it was the ferry to the island of Læsø. I opened the car door and got out on to the quay and said:

'So we're going to Læsø, are we?' But there

was no reply, and I turned and looked through the window to the back where my mother sat sideways leaning against the seat with her eyes closed, her body straight as an arrow and her lips in a tight line. Hansen was holding her arm and said loud enough for me to hear it:

'Do you feel bad? Shall we turn and go back? We can do this another day,' said Hansen. 'We can do it any time. I'm not going anywhere.'

'No, it's all right,' my mother said, 'I just felt a bit tired, and then there was a pain, but it will pass in a moment,' and I could hear how woollen, how restrained her voice was, as though it came from the bottom of a well, and then it struck me that I had forgotten why I was here, that the Teflon in my brain had displayed its slippery quality once more, and that made me feel so resigned and tired of myself that I stepped back to the car and spoke through the open door:

'Mother, I'm not coming. It's quite all right. Jesus. I can walk back to the summer house, I have done it before. Hell, I did so yesterday.' But she leaned forward in her seat with a groan, and opened the car door, clutched the sill and said:

'For God's sake, don't be so incredibly stupid. You're coming with us.' And I offered her my arm and she gripped my jacket firmly and slowly pulled herself up from the seat and came out, feet first, on to the quay and I would not let go, not for anything in the whole world, and she said:

'Arvid, that's enough, I'm on my feet now, it's fine,' and I said:

'Mother.' And then I started to cry, and I could not stop, and I did not care if Hansen could see it, and then I let go of her arm and ran around the car, pressed my forehead against the bonnet, and cried as I had never cried before, and hammered my hands ruthlessly against the hood of the Audi, then ran back, and just as ruthlessly slammed my hands against the shiny paintwork on the boot, and they could damned well stare if they wanted to, and I ran towards the ferry and leaned against the hull with the black water right down below me along the quay, and the water looked so icy cold, and I cried and turned from the ship and there was the young taxi driver knee deep in his embarrassed self, and he did not know where to look, because he was a young man still and had no idea what lay in store for him.

'All right, Arvid, that's enough. That will do,' said my mother, and I cried and she patted me clumsily on the shoulder, and then she patted me again, but harder this time, and said:

'That's enough, do you hear,' and then I finally stopped. Hansen came over and was clearly embarrassed on my behalf and we went on board. I did not have a ticket, but it was no problem, the ferry was never full this early in the morning. We crossed the gangway and my mother took out the worn brown purse she always kept in her handbag and paid the sum I cost.

23

We were standing hand in hand on the doorstep. It was a holiday camp. I had been there once before, but it was summer then, and the shadows did not stretch as far as they did now. We had come here to be alone. The cold was biting. The manager was a woman. She appeared from behind the main house, coming up the slope from the water in a blue quilted jacket, a bucket in one hand, there were fish in the bucket, perch I guessed, but I had not been fishing since I was a boy and remembered nothing about fish. The manager looked at my face and then at the girl standing next to me and saw that she was very young, looked back at me and said:

'You've booked a cabin?'

'Yes,' I said.

'I didn't expect you until tomorrow.'

'It was today,' I said.

'Was it?' she said.

'Yes, I believe it was,' I said.

'Well then, I guess it was,' she said. 'Not that it makes any difference, you are the only ones here, so you can have any cabin you like.'

I knew exactly which cabin I wanted. I told her the number. She opened the door, put down the bucket in the hall and I saw her take a key from the board on the wall that had several rows of small hooks, one number for each hook with the same number on a plastic chip attached to the key ring.

'There's firewood in the pile behind the cabin. Help yourself, and if there is anything else you need, just let me know.'

'We will,' I said, 'but I think we'll manage.'

'I'm driving to the shop tomorrow morning if there is anything you want me to get for you,' she said, and we both said thank you and if there was, we would come up.

We left the doorstep and crossed the yard in front of the house where the kiosk to the left was closed and the *Dagbladet* banner on either side of the hatch had been taken down, and walked past a tractor covered by a tarpaulin and on past several cabins scattered randomly among the trees and at last we reached the red timber cabin by the lake. Its foundation was raised on the bare rock and it stood tall on the side facing the water and low on the other side with a terrace and a door to the path. From the windows there was a view across the bay to the ridge on the opposite shore where spruce trees stood like columns right down to the waterline. At the far end of the bay there was a grocery store in the summer when the holiday guests were numerous. They could row there from all over the lake, and then the boats would lie gunnel to gunnel in a long line, a festive sight, a lady told me when I was here last, but of course the store was shut now.

★　★　☀

Some hours earlier we had taken the bus from Ankerløkka, a fine square at Akerselva in Oslo, now filled with student flats, but back then it still was a bus station, right across from St Jacob's Church, that was built of red brick like most churches in Oslo. It was pretty to look at standing there behind the naked trees that lined the road down towards the fairytale bridge and the river.

We caught the bus there, at Ankerløkka, and sat at the very back, and right on schedule the bus pulled slowly out into Storgata, and the wheels on the bus went round and round, as they do in the song. And then we drove through eastern Oslo, through Grønland and Gamlebyen and onwards along Mosseveien to the south, and we drove up the hills at Ljan Station or up Herregårdsveien, or a third route, and if we did I don't remember which, but definitely down towards

Hauketo where no high rises stood in those days, no terraced houses, more like it was in the countryside, in the woods. The diesel engine made the whole bus vibrate as we climbed higher and shuddering waves rose through our bodies, up our thighs to our stomachs and it was like an erotic sensation and she pressed both hands low down against her stomach and said:

'More, more, I want more,' and with a sensuous smile she closed her eyes. But then she took her hands away and laughed and blushed, and we sang the song of the Eighth Route Army softly to ourselves. We sang:

Soldier of the great people's army,
Don't forget our three commandments
Or the law of the eight rules
March, oh soldier, march.

and so on, and only a few passengers in the bus turned to look at us. We laughed at them a little, and the song too we laughed at, because here we were, sitting in a bus going through the woods in a country called Norway, where, of course, the class struggle was fought every single day, though not very visible to most of us, nor very fierce. But the song had a good rhythm, I mean, it was a march, wasn't it? And we tapped out the beat on the seats in front of us as we sang.

The red, almost burgundy-coloured bus with the pale blue lines along the windows drove on, towards the junction at the roadside café where Hauketo railway station lay to the right and the sign to Enebakk pointed left. And that was the way we went, and everything was as it had been the last time I was here, each bend in the road, all the bus stops with their shelters and rusty signs, and the kiosks were all closed now, and in their worn-down nakedness they stood against the bare forest and were filled to the brim with emptiness and time which had come and now was gone again: no Kvikklunsj bars on the shelves, no chocolate from Freia, no cigarette packs in their colourful rows: Winston, South State, Blue Master and Tiedemanns Teddy.

The weather had just changed from sleet and rain, now winter was coming, the air was cold, was clear, but inside the bus it was warm. We were ten passengers or even fewer on board, although on that day at this time of year it was the only bus. No proletarians, not one member of the working class came to spend their holiday in the cabins by the lake, not one worker from Spikerverket, not one family from the construction workers' union came to Loch Lysern, to fish in one of its many bays, to lie on their back on the thwarts of a rowing boat, the oars pointing to the sky and in their hands the workers' newspaper, *Arbeiderbladet*, or for no other reason than to stare into the blue after one more year of piecework and double shifts.

The others on the bus lived by the main road, so just the two of us were going all the way out to the holiday camp. We sat at the back of the bus and saw through the windows the frozen glittery dust whirling up in the slipstream of the bus, or in its wake, as after a boat. It hung like yellow curtains across the winding road and then was pulled aside by the wind after each bend before drifting in between the trees where it was gone.

'Are you happy?' she said.

'Yes,' I said.

'I am,' she said.

In the autumn and winter the bus stopped at the junction with the main road, Route 120, and did not go all the way up to the holiday camp, it was a surprise, we had to walk. And we did. The gravel road was hard as concrete in the sudden frost and the stubble fields were covered with icing. The road had frozen so solid it rang out beneath our boots with every step we took, like taps on a Spanish guitar, and it took us an hour to get there.

The main house was quiet when we

crossed the yard in the cold quiet air and we stood on the doorstep sending fans of misty breath from our mouths, and it was nearly dusk already and above the lake was a blue transparent light and a muted yellow light from the lamp above the door. We knocked and then cautiously rang the brass bell by the entrance, and a woman in a quilted blue jacket came from behind the house, on the path from the lake with a bucket in her hand.

★ ★ ★

I unlocked the door and let her in, and dropped the bag by the door and walked around the cabin to fetch firewood from the woodpile and walked back with my arms loaded up to my chin, but when I came in, there was already a fire burning and there was firewood in a basket in the corner. I wondered if I should feel embarrassed that she was the one who got the fire going. But I did not.

'Look what you can do,' I said.

'Girl Guides,' she said. 'I left only two years ago. Once a Guide, always a Guide,' she said and sang:

When the shadows softly gather
Ere we close our eyes in sleep

We would thank thee, holy Father,
For thy keep.

Keep our loved ones free from sorrow
And in bed with us tonight
Let's play our games till the morrow
Till the morning light

And she blushed as she always did, but I thought she was funny. She was funnier than I was.

*   *   *

We slept till late next morning. When I awoke the light was slowly coming; it was misty with a thin layer of white ice across the water to the other side of the bay as if someone had poured skimmed milk from a jug to let it freeze there. I looked at my watch and pulled my trousers on and my jumper I pulled over my head and closed the door softly on my way out and walked up to the main house. We were fresh out of tobacco, I had remembered the instant I woke up.

It was cold as hell on the way up, and past the tractor I saw her Ford in front of the kiosk shivering in the cold, pluming white fumes from the exhaust pipe. She was scraping ice off the windows on the other side of the car. I walked round and said:

'Jesus Christ, it's cold,' and she nodded and smiled and kept on scraping, and I stood there waiting, stepping from one leg to the other right behind her, my bare feet in my worn-out boots. At long last she was finished and threw the blue plastic ice scraper on to the passenger seat.

'We forgot the smokes,' I said. 'Would you mind?'

I fumbled with stiff fingers in a pocket and pulled out the pouch to show her which brand I wanted, in case she knew nothing about tobacco.

'Yes, of course,' she said, and I gave her the money she needed, and she looked at me and said: 'Aren't you freezing cold in that?' And I was. The knitted jumper I had on was the first the girl in the cabin had ever completed, and my skin was showing through the coarse stitches. I am not sure, but I thought the manager looked me over a little too closely, before she finally got in her car and drove across the yard and up the gravel track towards Route 120 and the shop.

★ ★ ★

I turned and walked down to the cottage.

When I opened the door, I rubbed my

hands, and I rubbed my ears until they burned. I went over to the stove and opened the little door and laid pieces of firewood inside so it looked in there like Stonehenge looked and pushed folded pages of *Dagbladet* between the logs. I put a match to the paper and let it burn almost down and then I did it two more times and left the door to the stove ajar and that did the trick. The wood was so dry that it took at once and the flames licked the logs. I closed the door fully and the stove started to rumble.

I heard her turn over in bed and could feel her eyes on my back. She said:

'Hello, boy, come back to bed.'

'I'm coming,' I said, and pulled off my jumper and trousers and lay down next to her under the duvet.

'Oh fuck, you're cold,' she said. 'Goddamnit you're cold,' she said, and she started to rub me hard all over my body, and then what happens happened, and afterwards we lay as we always did, shoulder to shoulder, hand in hand, and the warmth seeped into my body from her body, and I did not know how I kept warm all those years before I met her.

'Do you want to go rowing after breakfast?'

'There's ice on the water,' I said.

'But the ice is maybe not that thick?'

'Oh no, it's just a thin film.'

'Then it would be fun,' she said, and I thought so too.

'But first I want to lie here for a little while,' I said and closed my eyes, pressed myself against her and said: 'I went up to ask for some more cigarettes. We forgot to bring them. We only have the one pack, and that's not enough. I caught the manager just before she left.' I opened my eyes. 'Christ, did she stare at me, before she got in her car,' I said.

'She probably thought you looked good in that jumper.'

'Do you think so?'

'Of course. She could see right through those stitches.'

I laughed. 'Does it matter to you that she did?'

'Oh, no. That only means she and I have something in common. There's nothing wrong with that. She has nothing to do with us.'

I closed my eyes and was pleased with her answer, which was the answer I had wished for. I heard a rumbling from the stove, and the cabin was slowly warming up with the sweet scent of birch wood surrounding us, and the old timber smelled like something I had always known and always liked.

★ ★ ★

We were only there for the one night and would travel back from the bus stop on Route 120 later that afternoon, and it was really not much time, so we had to make the most of this day, and then I fell asleep, and we both slept, and we woke up and went to sleep again. Finally we were both fully awake and we got dressed and had breakfast and our heads were still fuzzy from sleep and we walked down to the water and tipped the rowing boat on to its keel and found the oars in the heather beneath the boat and together we dragged it down over the rocks to the water and pushed the boat in. We slid the oars on board and put a fishing rod under the thwarts. It was her fishing rod. We could hear the thin ice crunch. Carefully I stepped into the boat and sat down facing the shore and placed the oars in the rowlocks, and she followed and first she knelt on the stern thwart to push us off and she turned around and then we sat facing each other. She smiled.

'Why don't you row?' she said.

'Oh, sorry. Did you want to?' I said.

'It's fine. I can sit here and watch you toil. You just row.'

She was probably good at rowing. Canoeing was my thing. Red Indian. Rowing boat was cowboy.

'I'm the man,' I said and laughed.

'That's right,' she said and looked at me with narrow, almost dreamy eyes.

★ ★ ★

With each stroke the blades of the oars crunched the brittle ice and made ragged holes either side of the wide wake behind the boat. It sounded as if the ice was hitting back, like the polar ship *Fram* or even *Gjøa* on its way through the Northwest Passage, thump thump, but of course it didn't. It was plain sailing.

'This is fun,' she said. 'The sound of it, right? Is it hard?'

'No, no,' I said, 'it's plain sailing.'

She had two woollen vests on and an Icelandic sweater and a purple scarf around her neck and a leather cap on her head like the caps that fishermen wore in northern Norway, in Lofoten, and she had mittens on her hands. She was really well wrapped up, and her cheeks were flushed, and I wore three checked flannel shirts that used to be my father's, one over the other, and the jumper she had knitted and then my jacket and mittens. No cap. A cap was unmanly, and my ears grew quite cold, but not more than I could cope with.

'Shall we fish now?' she said.

'Why not. But then you throw the line, I'm busy with these oars.'

'That's fine with me.'

She pulled off her mittens and took the fishing rod from under the thwarts, it was fibreglass, bottle green, and swung it back and let the spinner loose and pressed her thumb softly against the lock, and with a swift, almost invisible flick she launched the bait. She clearly knew what she was doing, and the spinner pierced the ice with a crisp plop out on the lake.

The rowing boat was fibreglass, plastic, and rode too high on the water, and did not pick up the momentum a wooden boat would, when finally I fell into a rhythm I could handle. So I struggled to keep her on a straight course, and I was starting to sweat, and it annoyed me. I saw her face flush in the cold air and her eager eyes watching the shiny line and the white scrubbed water, and along the shore was a mist still drifting among the trees turning them into mythical creatures from some heathen past. A pale rose streak was floating above the red cabins along the bay and from behind the mist, the sun was breaking through, and why so annoyed, I thought, this is fine, this is so fine, you could not have wished for better, why shouldn't you sweat a little?

'Jesus, this boat is hard work,' I said.

'I know,' she said, 'they're like that, those plastic boats, they're really too light.' Then she got a bite. She jumped up and cried out: 'Got one! Fucking hell, we're going to get the bastard.' she yelled, and I had not heard her swear like this before, and I liked it, truly, it was exciting.

She let the fish thrash around before slowly reeling it in and lifting it carefully over the side.

'A perch,' she said, 'a big one.'

'Congratulations,' I said, and I meant it too, and she took a bow and dropped her head like maybe Chaplin would have done, or Pinocchio in the cartoon with his head on a string, and her cap tipped forward and she placed her left hand on her right breast and held the rod in an arc above her head and let the fish dangle there.

'A small fish in your honour, my sweet.'

I laughed and together we got the perch off the hook and tossed it into the bottom of the boat where it flapped about, and poor little fish, she said, and I took a stick that was lying there for that purpose and whacked it pretty hard on the head, and it flapped a little more and then lay still.

I straightened up. I could feel the sun on my back, the fog melting away, the ice melting. Her face was golden, her hair golden, and she lifted her face to the sun and closed her eyes in the dazzling light.

'Do I have a tan now?' she said.

I laughed again. 'You and I,' I said. 'Just you and I.'

'Isn't it fun,' she said and she smiled. I let the oars rest in the rowlocks. The water around the boat fell silent, and silently the cabin was floating up above the rocks and the smoke rose softly from the chimney, and how impossible it was to grasp that in the end something as fine as this could be ground into dust.

IV

VI

24

When we arrived at Læsø, we walked up to a small hotel in Vesterø harbour, where the ferry from the mainland docked. The old hotel was only a stone's throw from the quay, and my mother said that she was fine, she could walk the distance, she was no invalid for Christ's sake. The hotel had a view of the fishing port where seagulls whirled like a tornado above the masts and filled the sky. Their chests were so incredibly white it hurt our eyes when the sun was out. And there were all kinds of gulls and terns with their black cap and heavy grey gulls and orange, green and canvas-coloured sails on the boats and the red buoys flapping pennants in the wind and the nets spread fan-like along the quays.

'It's different here now,' my mother said.
'Different to when?' I said.
'To forty years ago.'
'You haven't been here for forty years?'
'No,' she said.
We went through the door to the hotel and put down our bags. I did not have a bag, but I was carrying my mother's blue one, and

Hansen had a bag. I had my father's clothes on and my damp jacket. I had to get it dry. It was cold on the inside. I might catch something, I might be ill.

My mother went up to the reception and took out her worn, ancient purse from her handbag. There was plenty of money in it, and she was spending it like she never had before; it looked conspicuous, and I did not like it. I heard her ask about a room for someone who had not booked in advance, and that someone, I guessed, was me, and there was no problem, not this time of year. She sounded terribly Danish though, and not like she normally did.

We went up to our rooms. My mother had to rest for an hour, and Hansen did too. I took the bottle of Calvados from my inside pocket and placed it on the bedside table and hung my jacket on a radiator below the window, it was good and warm, and the room was warm and I sat on the bed and stayed there looking out of the window to the harbour and thought about things that needed thinking about. But that didn't help me much.

I lay down on my back. The bed was soft. I closed my eyes and then time just vanished, and when I looked at my watch, an hour had passed. I put my steaming jacket on and went downstairs to eat with the others, and they were already there. I should have found it odd with Hansen sitting at the end of the table, and not my father. But I didn't, and when I realised, I felt guilty.

We ate by the window. I was really hungry. After a while my mother leaned over the table and looked out at the road. She did this twice, and the third time she stood up, took her coat from her chair and said:

'Right, time to go,' and Hansen stood up and this time I did not ask where we were going. I just left my food on the plate even though I was far from finished and stood up to join them. Where else could I go? In the road was a cab with the engine running. We sat as we did before. Me in the front next to the driver and the two others in the back. I don't know why it turned out that way, if it was something they decided that morning.

We drove south towards Byrum, one of three major villages on the island, and on both sides of the road were flat meadows framed by electric fences and stone walls and rows of low trees, shrub almost, and then by some taller trees depending on which farm the field belonged to, and now in November they looked cold and scrubbed clean.

We were approaching Byrum at speed. We saw the tower they had in that village come closer, and it was not a very tall tower, but easy to see in the flat landscape, like the tower of a knight's castle with its gun slits, and I do not know what the tower was used for in the past or what use they made of it now. Maybe they just liked to have something to look at. A strange thing in a Christian town, a thing of vanity pointing where only the church should point, and the church, I knew, was the oldest in the country, but we drove right past it and then south out of the village.

And we suddenly turned east almost heading back towards the coast, or so it seemed, but I guess the taxi driver knew something that I did not, and it was really not my problem, he could drive wherever he liked. It was a gravel road, the ground was dry, and in spite of the humid air, we could see a tail of dust whirling behind the car. Some kilometres further out on the plain we stopped. Of course, there was nothing *but* plains here. Off the road was a medium sized house built of yellow bricks with a narrow pointed roof and an attic room. It was not a very old house, nor was it new, not like they built them after the war. It was older than me. There were sheep behind the house. They had plenty of room to move about, but the whole flock stayed close to an outbuilding, a small barn I could barely see behind the yellow house, where no doubt the hay was laid out, now that the pastures were bare.

My mother climbed out of the car. Hansen stayed in his seat, so I stayed too. She walked a few steps towards the house, stopped and then came back, leaned into the car and picked up her bag from the back seat and took out an envelope before she slammed the door shut. She opened the envelope and shook out some black and white photographs, there were four of them. She leaned against the car door and spread the photos in her hand like cards in a poker game.

'What are we doing here?' I said.

'This is where your brother was born,' Hansen said. 'In this house.'

I bent forward and could clearly see the photographs through the window, and it was that house. It was her in two of them. She was sitting in the grass with a dog by her feet, a sheepdog, an ace of diamonds on its forehead, not that I knew much about dogs, but it was looking up at her, they were friends, the slightest hint and the dog would do whatever came into her head.

She was young, she had an apron wrapped loosely around her waist. She was very pretty. In the other photo she was sitting on the doorstep in front of the house next to a woman who was older than her. Not older like a mother is older, but maybe ten years older. The last two photos showed only the house, from two different angles. Someone had taken those photographs to remember exactly how the house looked.

She put the photographs back in the envelope, opened the door and placed the envelope on the seat in the back and looked over at Hansen. Hansen nodded and smiled. She took a deep breath, closed the car door and started to walk towards the house, a little shaky on her feet, I thought.

Once she was there, she stood for at least one minute before she knocked on the door, and then she waited, and no one came. She turned and looked at us, and with her palms up she shook her head, and Hansen just nodded and smiled. So again she knocked, much harder now, and she waited, and someone came to open the door, an elderly woman, she was older than my mother, maybe seventy. They stood facing each other. They started to talk, but I could not hear what they were saying, they were too far away.

'Are we supposed to just sit here in the car?' I said.

'I guess we'll sit here for as long as it takes,' Hansen said.

'All right,' I said.

They stood on the doorstep and the sun hit

the car in a flash through the windscreen and was gone, and the taxi driver sat smoking with the window ajar, a Prince cigarette it was, and I turned away from the stinging smoke.

* * *

'I remember you,' my mother said. 'You're Ingrid. Do you remember me?'

The woman stood with her right elbow leaning stiffly against the door frame and her fist slightly clenched in the air in a way I would bet she had done her whole life long. She looked closely at my mother's face, left the door frame to support itself, took two steps back and pulled a pair of glasses from her apron pocket.

'Yes,' she said. 'I remember you. I remember your name. You were here, not long after the war. Only a few years. We didn't look then like we do now,' she smiled. 'But maybe we're still the same.'

'Maybe not,' my mother said.

'You're probably right, but please, won't you come in?'

'I would like that,' my mother said.

She walked behind the old woman into the hall and bent down to undo the shiny zip on her ankle boots, and it took some effort, and the woman called Ingrid said: 'That's how you used to do it back then, you were pregnant, just keep them on, it's a dry day, it doesn't matter, I'll just sweep the floor.'

She smiled. 'I'll make some coffee,' she said and went out into the kitchen. There were two gas rings on the counter, and she lit the one and placed on it a shiny kettle with a whistle on the spout. My mother entered the living room. It was not like before. It looked like an old woman's living room. No matter who you were when you were young, the day would come when everything was in its place, the knick-knacks and lace tablecloths, the little china dogs and the china shepherd boy by the mill wheel somewhere in the Alps, and on the wall in their frames, the guardian angel watching over the little girl with blonde plaits leaning too far out over the water to catch a fish, or whatever it was in the brook. On the windowsill there were pots of geraniums and they had been there for a long time already and were white and red.

My mother unbuttoned her coat and pulled it slightly off her shoulders before she sat down at the coffee table and looked out of the window towards the outbuilding where the sheep stood silent, looking heavy, with their heads against the wall like they did back then, in the autumn, in the winter, in the sun and in the snow. In the summer they moved out to the heather on the heath and grazed there. They could go wherever they pleased, but always came back in the evening, like goats do on the mountain pastures in Norway.

Ingrid entered with coffee in a china pot and cups on a tray.

'You still have sheep,' my mother said.

'It seems I can't give it up. We've had sheep here for as long as I can remember. Or I have, but I manage fine. Haulier Karlsen died young, you know.' She still referred to her husband as *haulier* Karlsen, as she did forty years ago.

Ingrid sat down on the sofa with her back to the window.

'A neighbour helps me at lambing time, and if I am in distress I do have the telephone,' she said and smiled. 'But of course, I have to stop soon.' She placed a cup on the table in front of my mother. She waited. She was not impatient. She leaned forward and poured the double-roasted coffee into the cup and the aroma was overwhelming.

'I wanted to see you one more time,' my mother said. 'I made up my mind only a few days ago. It felt like the right thing to do.'

'Ah, but that suits me fine,' Ingrid said, 'I don't have many visitors. Only my son every now and then. He lives in the town across the water. I thought about you a great deal in the first years. But then it went away.' Her voice was calm and careful so the words would not come out wrong.

'I thought a great deal about you, too. Sometimes you were all I had. We would meet again, I used to think, but nothing ever came of it, even though I was home so many times,' my mother said and she pointed to what she thought was the mainland. It was not of course, but she said:

'This house is where the rest of my life began. Or where the first part ended. Or both. You were. It felt safe here, no place could have been better, and I would have loved to stay, but when he was a year old, I had to go to Norway. I thought I had no choice. But I did.' And then my mother cried with her head on her knees. 'It did not turn out as I had imagined,' she said, 'as I had hoped, no, it did not,' she said harshly, 'and now I am ill'.

Ingrid was still smiling. 'Is it serious?' she said.

'It is,' my mother said. 'At least *they* seem to think so.'

'I'm sorry to hear that,' Ingrid said. 'Shall we go for a walk? After the coffee? Are you up to it?'

'Yes, I am.'

They drank the coffee. They smiled at each other, my mother dried her eyes. It was good to sit there, it was warm, and then for a moment she thought, I am really not up to it.

'Was that him in the car? It would be interesting to see how he turned out, now that he's a grown-up.'

'No, the one out there is his brother. He's younger.'

'And he's not coming inside?'

'He's not coming inside. He's thirty-seven years old, but I wouldn't call him a grown-up. That would be an exaggeration. He's getting a divorce. I don't know what to do with him. And my friend, Hansen, too, is in the taxi. He came, well, as a friend. He doesn't mind waiting.'

'Won't the taxi be expensive?'

'We've agreed on a price, it's all right.'

'That's good to hear,' Ingrid said and stood up and went out into the hall and put on her coat, and my mother followed and her body felt heavy, unwilling.

'Talking comes easier when you walk,' Ingrid said, and my mother said she was probably right.

Ingrid tied a scarf around her head. 'It's vile outside,' she said, 'you need something to cover your head.' She pulled a scarf down from a shelf, a white one with pink flowers, like the scarves my mother had seen old Russian women wear, and I suppose that is what I am, she thought. An old woman.

★ ★ ★

The door opened and they stepped outside, their scarves tight around their heads, and the old woman pulled the door behind her, turned and looked towards the car where we were sitting, and for some reason she locked the door, but I don't think it had anything to do with us. They came down with their hands in their coat pockets and started to walk, away from the taxi across the plain, and it was not easy for me to imagine what they said to each other.

When they were about twenty metres away, Hansen opened the door on his side of the car, got out and walked in the opposite direction. I followed him.

'Are your legs stiff?' I said.

'Yes,' he said.

'Mine too.'

We walked a while, I turned up the collar of my jacket and the sky was grey above us, weighing our heads down and the air was moist and sticky against our faces and pressed at my temples. After some time I pulled the tobacco pouch from my pocket and rolled a cigarette, then I rolled another and offered it to Hansen.

'Thanks,' he said, 'I don't mind if I do,' and I lit them both and we smoked and damnit, it tasted good.

'What do you think they're talking about?' I said.

'That's not hard to guess,' said Hansen. 'They're talking about her time here when your brother was born. The one who came before you. This is where it happened, you know.'

'I know. You just told me. In a way I have always known it,' I said, 'but I just couldn't picture it, no one told me anything.'

'No, I don't suppose they did. Maybe they should have.'

'Yes,' I said. And then I said: 'Do you think they're talking about me too?'

'Probably not.'

'No, I don't suppose they are,' I said.

Hansen did not really want to talk, so we walked on in silence, and the plain was flat as only Danish plains can be. Once, a long time ago, someone must have run amok with an iron round here.

Across the plain was a cluster of houses. A couple of them had roofs covered in dried seaweed. There were trees planted in a circle around the houses; they were still small, the trees, pine and spruce, and around the circle we walked and then back the way we had come. As we did not walk fast time barely touched us. Tick tick, it softly said. Like a taxi meter. When we reached the car, we quickly climbed in and the taxi driver had kept the engine running to keep it warm. I looked at the petrol gauge, but the needle showed half full and maybe more.

And then they came walking back along the road, arm in arm, scarf to scarf, slightly bent against the damp wind. They stopped in front of the house, still arm in arm, or rather, hand in hand, and still there were things to be said, for they walked up to the house together and were gone behind the door, and we sat in the car waiting, each huddled against our corner, and fifteen minutes later she came down from the house, alone, with a small parcel in her hand.

★ ★ ★

After dinner at the hotel, I went up to my room to fetch the bottle of Calvados from the bedside table and three plastic cups and came back down again. My mother and Hansen were still sitting at the table, I placed the bottle and the cups in front of them. They were both smoking. It was dark outside. They looked at each other, and then my mother looked at me and smiled faintly, without enthusiasm, but she didn't look sceptical either. I poured Calvados into the plastic cups, and Hansen raised his and said:

'*Arch of Triumph* then, isn't it,' and my mother raised hers and said:

'*Arch of Triumph*, a toast to Boris and Ravic, God bless them both,' and they laughed, and I raised my cup too, and I took a sip. The taste was strong and good and much better than the taste of whisky. I could feel the alcohol glowing in my stomach, and Hansen's bass made everything vibrate.

'Jesus Christ,' he said, 'that was good booze.'

'One more,' I said and raised the bottle, but Hansen shook his head, and my mother said:

'That'll do for today. I'm going upstairs. See you in the morning.'

'Ditto,' Hansen said, and I knew that word and I knew what it meant, so then he too would go upstairs, and he did, and together they climbed to the first floor and left me at the table. I poured another shot and drank the yellow liquid in small sips as I looked down to the harbour through the window and saw the lights along the quays, and in some boats the lights were burning and there were lamps along the walkway. I stood up, took my reefer jacket from the chair, stuck the bottle in my inside pocket, and brought the cup with me and went down to the harbour and on to one of the quays where the fishing boats lay one after another. I did not stop until I was all the way out and I stood there listening to the soft and jingly sound of the waves against the concrete in the dark. I filled my cup almost to the brim and walked slowly back while I drank. I felt good, almost happy. It was the alcohol, I knew that, but it did not matter.

25

Hansen was not yet awake, so just the two of us were standing on the beach facing west, towards the mainland. The weather had changed, and it was glitteringly cold, and the morning light was well on its way. It was well below zero and the air was bright as it sometimes is in the autumn; transparent, as if a magnifying glass had been lowered from the sky. Through the glass we could see the town on the mainland come into focus with its faint, rust-coloured skyline to the north and the south, and in the midst of it the church tower rose high. On days with no mist you could stand on the ridge behind the town and see across the water to the beach where we were standing now.

I could just make out the top of the old grain silo, which was concrete grey and massive with the red *dlg* logo floating high above the harbour, but of course we could not see the letters from here. The silo was empty now, nothing but hollow echoes and multitudes of cubic metres black as coal from top to bottom. Everything was changing, the whole town was. There were car-free zones and more shops than before, there were more pubs, more ferries packed with drunken Norwegians and drunken Swedes.

I half turned and looked at her. The air was clear and the wind cut our faces. With her left hand she held her coat tight at her throat, with the right she held her cigarette in a hollow between gloved fingers to shield it from the wind, and the wind whipped her hair in curly circles, and it was still dark, but the grey streaks were easier to see than even yesterday.

I had my reefer jacket on and was holding my cigarette between naked fingers. My ears were probably white as chalk now and my fingers were slowly turning blue. They felt so cold I thought they might crack, and my nails ached, and then I could not take it any more and threw my half-smoked cigarette on the hard, frozen sand. I stuck my hands in my pockets and clenched them hard in there and opened them several times. My right hand felt much better now. Perhaps because it was numb. My swollen cheek burned in the cold.

'Didn't you bring any gloves or mittens?'

'No,' I said.

'You're a bit scatterbrained,' she said and touched my shoulder gently with hers and it made me so happy. 'You always have been,' she said.

'I know,' I said. 'I've been like that since I was little.'

'I'm afraid I don't have an extra pair. I brought just the one pair with me.'

'That's all right. I'll keep them warm in my pockets.'

'But then you won't be able to smoke that cigarette.'

'Mother, I don't have to smoke all the time.'

'No, of course not. One ought to give it up, really. I ought to.' And she fell silent and simply stared into the distance and then she said: 'Christ, there's no point in quitting now.'

I should have said the right thing just then, but I did not know what that would be, if such a thing existed, I did not think so, and those who said it did, knew nothing. So I said the first thing that came into my head.

'Are you afraid?' I said.

'What of?' she said and turned sharply and looked me in the face for the first time since we came down here. I could feel my face turn red, and I stared at the ground.

'Do you think I'm afraid of dying?' she said.

'I don't know,' I said. 'Are you?'

'No,' she said, 'I'm not afraid of dying. But damnit, I don't want to die now.' She turned back and took a deep drag of her cigarette, and she stared at the coast across the waves and furiously blew smoke towards the waterline.

It was true, she was not afraid of anything that I could think of, but I knew there were a few things she wanted to see before she died, wanted to experience, of course everybody felt that way, but she really wanted to see the Soviet Union collapse, now that the Wall had come down. To be a part of that and what would follow, to see Gorbachev triumph or step down and say the whole thing had gone too far, which was not improbable; but in any case it would be bitter if she did not get to live through it and I, too, wanted to see it all, and probably I would, but when it came to dying, I was scared. Not of *being* dead, that I could not comprehend, to be nothing was impossible to grasp and therefore really nothing to be scared of, but the dying *itself* I could comprehend, the very instant when you know that now comes what you have always feared, and you suddenly realise that every chance of being the person you really wanted to be, is gone for ever, and the one you were, is the one those around you will remember. Then that must feel like someone's strong hands slowly tightening their grip around your neck until you can breathe no more, and not at all as when a door is slowly pushed open and bright light comes streaming out from the inside and a woman or a man you have always known and always liked, maybe always loved, leans out and gently takes your hand and leads you in to a place of rest, so mild and so fine, from eternity to eternity.

'Why don't we go back up?' I said.

'I want to stay here for a bit. You go back,' she said, 'I will come later.'

'Are you sure?' I said.

'Yes, of course I'm sure,' she said, but I felt it would be wrong of me to leave, so I stayed, and she said:

'Be off with you then.' So I had to go.

'All right,' I said.

I turned and walked up towards the harbour and the hotel with the wind in my back. A little further along the path through the sand I stopped, turned and saw her still standing there facing the town across the water, and then I left the path and walked in between the dunes, which could hardly be called dunes, but that was what I called them when I was little. They were more like mounds of sand and marram grass that held the sand together in an intricate net, and there was shelter at the back of the biggest mound, and the wind did not blow as hard as it did on the beach, and it did not feel as cold. I raised my hands to my ears and rubbed them.

I sat down with my back against the mound. I let my head sink into my jacket before I pulled my sleeves over my hands and folded my arms and leaned my head against my knees.

After some time I rolled over and crawled on my knees and elbows to the edge of the mound and from there I looked down towards the beach. She still stood facing the water. The wind blew harder now and whipped the foam from the crest of one wave to another. It was really something. I shuttled back and sat down as before. I stared down at the sand. There was not much to look at. I am thirty-seven years old, I thought. The Wall has fallen. And here I sit.

After what I hoped was fifteen minutes or more, I did the same thing again, rolled over and crawled on my elbows and knees to the edge of the mound and looked towards the beach. She was on her knees now. It looked strange.

I lay like this for a few moments to see if she would stand up, but she didn't. I crawled back and leaned against the mound, squeezed my eyes shut and tried to concentrate. I was searching for something very important, a very special thing, but no matter how hard I tried, I could not find it. I pulled some straws from a cluster of marram grass and put them in my mouth and started chewing. They were hard and sharp and cut my tongue, and I took more, a fistful, and stuffed them in my mouth and chewed them while I sat there, waiting for my mother to stand up and come to me.

We do hope that you have enjoyed reading this large print book.

Did you know that all of our titles are available for purchase?

We publish a wide range of high quality large print books including:
Romances, Mysteries, Classics
General Fiction
Non Fiction and Westerns

Special interest titles available in large print are:
The Little Oxford Dictionary
Music Book
Song Book
Hymn Book
Service Book

Also available from us courtesy of Oxford University Press:
Young Readers' Dictionary
(large print edition)
Young Readers' Thesaurus
(large print edition)

For further information or a free brochure, please contact us at:
Ulverscroft Large Print Books Ltd.,
The Green, Bradgate Road, Anstey,
Leicester, LE7 7FU, England.
Tel: (00 44) 0116 236 4325
Fax: (00 44) 0116 234 0205